summer

SUE WALLMAN

Scholastic Children's Books
An imprint of Scholastic Ltd
Euston House, 24 Eversholt Street, London, NW1 1DB, UK
Registered office: Westfield Road, Southam, Warwickshire, CV47 0RA
SCHOLASTIC and associated logos are trademarks and/or
registered trademarks of Scholastic Inc.

First published in the UK by Scholastic Ltd, 2016

ISBN 978 1407 16536 3

A CIP catalogue record for this book
is available from the British Library.

Printed by CPI Group (UK) Ltd, Croydon, CR0 4YY
Papers used by Scholastic Children's Books are made
from wood grown in sustainable forests.

5 7 9 10 8 6 4

www.scholastic.co.uk

To my sister, Clare, who inspires me

one

Yew Tree House, last summer

My sister doesn't use the word *disappear* but that's what she means. She squats barefooted by the side of the swimming pool and says, "Go to your room, Skye, and stay there until I say."

She's had an argument with someone who's on his way over, and she says it'll be easier to sort out if I'm not around. I'm not impressed. Too much of the summer has been about keeping out of the way when she's on the phone or meeting her new friends.

"Why can't I carry on swimming?" I ask her. "You have the whole house to yourself until Mum's back." I place my elbows on the smooth stone that edges the pool and adjust my goggles. Through the black-tinted lenses, she looks as if she's in an old film, her face flawless and her figure perfect in shorts and a tie-waist top. "I think you've forgotten this is my house too," I say to her glossy two-colour toenails.

"Get out of the pool," says Luisa. She grabs the towel and my clothes that I dumped on the paving slabs. "This guy's being an idiot and I don't want you involved. I don't know how he found out where I live, but he'll be here soon. Please."

The edge in her voice makes me lever myself out of the pool without any more fuss, and pull off my goggles. "What was the argument about?" I ask as I take the towel from her, flip it round my shoulders and use the corner to wipe water from my face.

She shoves the clothes at me. "It's more of a misunderstanding."

We hear a car swerve on to the driveway at the front of the house, the crunch of the gravel, the slam of a car door and the faint ring of the doorbell. Luisa doesn't move.

I stamp a perfect footprint on to the warm paving stones and watch it fade before my eyes. "Are you going to let him in?" I ask.

"Maybe I'll pretend I'm not here," she says.

"Is the misunderstanding something to do with Nico?" This summer would be so much better if Luisa wasn't going out with him.

She checks her mobile. "Sort of."

We hear footsteps on the gravel and Luisa looks at me. There's panic in her eyes. The side gate's not locked. There used to be a combination lock on it but it broke.

"Quick," she says. "You'll have to go into the changing room instead." She pushes me towards the little building next to the pool. "Don't come out until it's over. Promise?" She squeezes my shoulders and I nod; then I'm inside and she's slammed the door behind me.

My eyes take a couple of seconds to adjust to the gloom, and my nose to the smell of chlorine and plug-in pine air freshener. I place my clothes and goggles on the nearer of the two wicker chairs. I could have a long shower. Spend a while letting the conditioner soak in and use up all the hot water. I could flip through the wrinkled magazine that's been left on the little table to dry out, but I wouldn't be able to concentrate. I want to know what's going on.

I go back towards the door and stand next to the gap where it doesn't quite meet the door frame.

"Don't try to intimidate me," I hear Luisa say. She's speaking in her I'm-the-eldest-and-I'm-in-charge voice. Very slowly, I push down on the door handle. When I can't move it down any further, I push gently against the door and open it a crack. She's lying on a sunlounger on the other side of the pool, tanned legs bent, doing something on her phone. "Just say what you want to say, then leave."

I can't see the person from this angle. I hope he's having trouble with the gate to the pool area. His words aren't clear; then there's the *click-clack* of the gate as it closes, and he says loudly, "I've given you chances. I warned you. I've been very reasonable."

I inch the door open further and I see him, striding towards Luisa. Black jeans, tight green T-shirt, dark glasses, older than her and Nico. He looks vaguely familiar.

What did he warn her about?

Luisa shrinks away from him, and my heart speeds up. What am I going to do if things get ugly? I don't have a phone on me. If I run to get help at the farm, I'll have to go past him.

"You're pathetic," says Luisa.

No, Lu. Please don't wind him up.

He swears close up to her face and mutters something about respect. Luisa scrunches up her eyes, and I close mine too.

Make him go away.

There's a cracking, smashing sound, closely followed by a scream. I open my eyes. Luisa is off the sunlounger, staring at something on the paving stones. "Look what you've done to my phone!" she yells.

She needs to get rid of him. Now he's gripping the top of her arm.

"Let go of me," Luisa shouts. Her voice is wavy. Fear flutters in my throat.

"You're ruining everything," he says.

She bites him, and he swears. I know as my heart thumps out of control, just know, that he's about to do something terrible. I back away from the door, into a wall.

4

Time bends out of shape into slow and confusing motion as my mind tells me to do something but my body doesn't respond. *Don't come out until it's over* says a voice in my head. I slide down the wall on to the dusty tiles, push my face into my knees and breathe in the chlorine from my skin. There are shouts. An ear-splitting scream. A thud. A splash. A dog barking in the distance. Birds cawing.

two

Now

I need to get away. But maybe a holiday for bereaved kids isn't the answer.

Mum turns into the driveway of Morley Hill Activity and Adventure Centre, and I remove my earphones. "This looks lovely, Skye," she says. She'd have said that even if the place resembled a refugee camp, because she wants this holiday to work out.

From the outside, the centre looks pretty much as it does on the website, although the colours aren't as brochure-bright. The grounds are tucked away behind a fence but I can see some of the buildings. There are two main styles going on: fake wooden chalet and budget hotel chain.

As the car crunches up the thick gravel drive, a dog barks far away somewhere and Mum launches into a frenzy of instructions. "Text me at least once a day, won't you? I hope you'll make the most of having counsellors around. Try and go to the optional talks. Are you sure you packed your phone charger?"

I nod in the right places and discover I have a new phobia: dogs barking. More specifically, the sound of a dog barking in the distance. Inside the reception building there are four check-in desks, two of them open for business. My letter says to register at Yellow Desk. The woman there (short grey hair, old but not that old, unfortunate choice of pink glasses) beams enthusiastically, introduces herself as Pippa and says she's in charge of the Bereaved Aid for Kids charity, that everyone calls BAK-up because its tagline is *Providing great backup for those who need it most*. She ticks me off a list, tells me my accommodation block is D and my room number is four, and the code for the entry door. That should be it, except Mum insists on checking she has the correct emergency numbers in her phone, and rereads the parental consent forms one last time before handing them over.

It means I'm still there when a small skinny girl registers after me. She was dropped by taxi right outside the door. She speaks so quietly I don't catch her name until Pippa searches through her list and says, "Ah, Fay, one of your room-mates is right here." She holds out an arm towards me. "Skye, meet Fay."

"Hi. Yes. I'm Fay." She speaks in short breathy bursts, and does a lot of blinking. Her navy-and-white polka dot sundress emphasizes her flat chest, and she has sunburn-edged strap marks from another top. "I'm so nervous about this holiday. I'm rubbish at any sport."

"Really?" I say, acting surprised, even though she looks completely like she'd be rubbish.

She over-smiles and tugs at her ponytail. If she's on this holiday she must be fifteen or sixteen, but it's hard to believe. "Let's team up!"

I wonder who died in Fay's life.

When I was offered a place on this holiday camp a few months ago, it seemed like a great idea. Six days and five nights away from everyone. Back-to-back activities, so there'd be little time to think about the stuff in my head. Fully funded. Perfect, given the family finances. Until today I conveniently ignored the fact that every person in the group would have had someone close to them die. That I'd have to interact with them and be nice.

"I'll round up an instructor to show you to your room," says Pippa.

"You go ahead," I say to Fay. "I have to say goodbye to Mum."

Two people hurt in one go. I don't want to be lumped together with Fay. Not straight away. And I know Mum wants to see our room, but I'm doing her a favour. Seriously. She'll find it hard to leave otherwise. After seeing the room, she'll want to do a tour of the grounds, and then she'll want to hang around so she can meet the other people in the group.

Fay sets off with a twenty-something in a yellow T-shirt. All instructors for our group wear yellow T-shirts, Pippa explains. There are three separate groups at the centre this week. Yellow, Blue and Red. The Reds, the biggest group, arrived yesterday. They're teenagers from some music organization. In the mornings they practise their instruments in the hall. Blues are normal kids whose parents booked them into summer camp.

Yellow is the colour of bereaved teenagers. The colour that doesn't suit anyone.

I leave my suitcase in the reception building, near Pippa's desk, and walk with Mum to the car. We have a lingering hug and I let her squeeze me too tightly, and I breathe in floral perfume fumes without choking. She climbs into the car, but she can't drive off yet, because another car is inching its way up the driveway and there's no room to pass. It means we have to chat through the open car window.

"I hope you have a fabulous time," Mum says. "It's a great opportunity." She has high hopes that I'll return home a better person.

"Yeah."

I accidentally catch the eye of a boy in the front passenger seat of the car. Dark eyes, brown skin, wild black hair, and a pale blue polo shirt collar. He gives a little wave. To me. There's no one else around, so it has to be to me. By the time I think of waving back, the car's moved on, towards a parking space.

Mum's playing about with the satnav. She thinks I don't know what she's doing. We're not that far from Pitford here. She's making sure her route home doesn't take her anywhere near our old house, just like she did on the way here. She reads her self-help books and bangs on about closure but she can't walk the talk any more than I can.

I take a deep breath but the image of the swimming pool at Yew Tree House is already there in my head. The red water. Luisa underneath the surface, face down, her hair fanned out like seaweed.

"I'd better go, while the drive is clear," says Mum. "I love you."

"I love you too," I say. It's easier to be the daughter she wants me to be when I know she's leaving. I watch until the car disappears on to the main road and ignore the hollow feeling in my stomach.

The reception area is busier when I walk back in. There are people registering, and the Reds are gathering for an outing with full-on shrieks and shouts. It means I can loiter for a bit before I have to find room D4 and hang out with Fay.

The walls are covered with giant photos of smiling kids in helmets, kids dangling from ropes or in life jackets on rafts. There are smaller photos of groups with school names underneath, everyone throwing shapes and doing peace signs.

They remind me of a photo that's tucked away in a still-to-be-unpacked box in our new flat, taken on the school residential we did in the Isle of Wight when I was eleven. We swam, did obstacle courses, played endless games of rounders, and I got to kiss Jay Morris in a game of forfeits. I was a super-sporty kid back then. People wanted me on their team. Jay Morris wasn't embarrassed to be kissed by me.

When I go to retrieve my suitcase, Pippa's registering the boy I saw in the car. His spotless polo shirt, with massive designer logo, is a mismatch with his scruffy shorts. Trying too hard to be different. Before Pippa can pair us up, I grab my suitcase while she's not looking. But as I walk away I feel his gaze on me, and rearrange my baggy top, shifting it downwards over my denimed thighs.

I manage to find D4 with the assistance of a map on the wall of the reception building illustrating what to do in the event of fire. It's not hard. There are only four accommodation blocks, one after the other, each with a separate entrance. After trying the door handle of D4 and finding it locked, I knock and there's a short wait and some clumsy attempts at unlocking it before it opens.

"Hi!" says Fay. "Welcome to our room."

It's mostly – one wall, the curtains and the duvet covers – orange. There are three single beds in a row, closer to one another than I'd have liked. On the wall there's a metal-framed map of the site. The en-suite bathroom is white and gleaming, though the non-slip rubber mat, grey floor and extra handrails make me think of hospitals.

Fay has already taken the bed under the window, and placed on her pillow a soft-toy rabbit that looks as if it's been run over several times. I take the bed nearest the bathroom, and furthest away from her. We each have a small wooden chest of drawers by our beds, and a shelf to place our suitcases on in the narrow gap between the ends of our beds and the wall. I unpack some of my things and place them in my chest of drawers while Fay talks about her journey as if I might be interested in coaches and taxis.

"I think it'll be all right here," I cut in and tell her. "If it's not, it's only six days and we're almost halfway through the first one."

She smiles and doesn't feel the need to yabber on quite so much after that. When she goes to arrange her toiletries in the bathroom, I find my phone and settle myself on the bed, up against the headboard with a pillow behind my back. I log on to the free wifi and flick through various sites. But I end up, like I usually do, scrolling through my photos of Luisa.

three

When somebody dies, you view photos of them in a different way. You want a reminder of how they looked, but you also search for hidden truths in their eyes, answers to questions you can no longer ask them.

My favourite photo of Luisa is her star-jumping into the pool at Yew Tree House, but only she and the cloudless sky are in the shot. The sun is shimmering, her hair is half out of her ponytail and she's laughing. It was taken a couple of years ago by Toby, our neighbour at the farm next door. It was just before they broke up. He must have known his days were numbered. Even I knew that he couldn't contain her for ever.

I enlarge the photo on my phone so that I can study

Luisa's face. Happy, carefree and beautiful. It still seems impossible that she's dead when she was once so in-your-face alive.

Fay comes out of the bathroom and informs me that there are three shelves in there and she hopes it's OK but she's taken the bottom one because she's not very tall.

She looks over my shoulder, tilting her head. Not even trying to hide that she's looking at my screen. I exit my photos. They're private.

"I'll show you a photo of me and my dad," says Fay.

Lucky me.

She unzips an inside pocket of her suitcase and brings over a silver frame. She polishes it on her T-shirt before handing it to me. It was taken in a restaurant, the two of them scrunched together for the photo. Her dad is a thin man without much hair. He has a serious face and small, dark eyes, like Fay.

"You look like him."

"Thanks. Everyone says that," says Fay. "I try to pretend he's not dead. I tell myself he's working as a professor on the other side of the world."

"Does it help?" I ask as I hand the frame back to her.

"A bit," says Fay. She polishes it again before zipping it away.

Lunch is various salads followed by a chocolate brownie with a crispy crust and a squishy inside. The best type. We sit at two long tables in what's called the yellow dining

14

room because it's been assigned to us, the Yellow Group. In actual fact, the walls are a dreary mushroom-soup colour. Apart from breakfast, which is in the main dining room, this is where we eat and have exclusively Yellow activities. Everywhere else is multicoloured territory.

Our group is missing a member. The third girl in our room is arriving late by train and Pippa has gone to pick her up. I sit next to Fay, who flicks her salad round the plate and talks in her little kid's voice about how she's in a gifted student programme.

She says she wants to be a doctor, and when she starts up about work experience in hospitals, I can't help thinking about Oscar, my brother. Nine years old with four big operations behind him. I push my chair backwards with a loud scrape, and go to select another brownie.

Pippa comes back towards the end of lunch with our room-mate. She has short black hair, expensive green headphones round her neck, tight jeans and a vest top that clings in the right places. Multiple earrings follow the curve of one ear. The other is bare. Her name is Danielle.

A short while later, a member of the catering staff comes in to take plates away and Pippa stands up and clinks a piece of cutlery against her glass for attention. "Now that everyone's arrived, I'd like to officially welcome you all to Morley Hill. This holiday has been made possible by BAK-up, and each of you is coming to terms with losing someone special in your lives. Moving on is a difficult but necessary stage of bereavement and we hope this week will help. That's why our holiday camp is called *Getting on with Your Life*."

It is? I must have skim-read that part of the letter. I picture Pippa in different-coloured glasses as she tells us that attendance at various workshops throughout the week is optional but thoroughly recommended. Regular brown glasses would be my choice for her.

"Let's introduce ourselves. Say where you're from and what you're looking forward to most about this week. It could be . . . a specific activity, making friends, being with people who understand what you're going through. I'm not going to ask you to talk about what brought you here. You yourselves can decide when you're ready to do that." She swivels round, giving us all a chance to see her calm counsellory smile.

I imagine a hideous getting-to-know-you game where we're each given a list of everyone's names and another list with the relationship to their dead person and how they died, and we have to mingle and match everyone up.

"Who wants to go first?" asks Pippa.

A boy on the other table raises his arm. He has longish blond hair, tanned skin and the sleeves of his graffiti art T-shirt are tight round bulgy muscles. Boy-band material. He'd be the laid-back one with a tragic past. "I'm Joe," he says. "I come from Cornwall. I'm into surfing and being outdoors, so this holiday was a no-brainer for me. I'm looking forward to hanging out with all of you. It's going to be fun."

A couple of people clap, but I don't know why.

Fay's next. She kicks off with how her dad died in a car crash three years ago. How she was sitting in the front passenger seat and nearly died too. I don't want to listen. She goes on and on about how much she misses him and I look out of the window at the grass, trees, flower beds and winding paths. There's a swimming pool somewhere in the grounds. I picture myself easing on a swimming hat and lowering my goggles on to my face; then I take a deep breath. Without closing my eyes, I imagine myself diving into a deep pool of turquoise water and swimming underwater as far as I can, until my lungs are nearly exploding.

I'm aware that the boy in the pale blue polo shirt is looking at me. I exhale abruptly. A bit too loudly. Other people look at me. Fay trails off, sparing us any more details about her stay in hospital, and the boy grins. Properly, so that I see he has great teeth.

"How about you, Brandon?" says Pippa, and he looks from me to her.

"Er, yes, so I'm Brandon," he says. "I'm from London, and I'm here because my mum made me come."

There are a few laughs. Not from me.

Pippa nods. "I hope you'll have a good time."

He gives a small shrug. The polite sort.

Danielle plays with one of her earrings as she speaks. She says she's from a village we'll never have heard of. "What I'm looking forward to this week is a break from my dad." Next to me, Fay flinches.

Then it's my turn. "My name's Skye and I live near London."

But that's not where I'm from.

The button on the waistband of my jeans is too tight. I need to wriggle into a better position so it doesn't dig into me so much. "I'm here because I wanted a holiday," I say. "I'm looking forward to the high ropes and jumping from the tower."

"You can have your first adrenaline rush later today," says Pippa. "The high-rope session is at four o'clock."

Some people start talking about the high ropes, and Pippa waits for a while before calling for quiet. Once you get past those glasses, she seems relatively normal, and not too teacherish.

She keeps on round the group with the introductions. There are twelve of us. At the end, she checks her watch and says, "You now have exclusive use of the swimming pool until three. I'll see you later at the high-ropes course."

Fay, Danielle and I change into our swimming stuff in our room, in mostly awkward silence, and wind towels round ourselves for the walk to the pool.

"This was my dad's swimming towel," says Fay. She secures it against her waist with one hand and holds the other arm out so we can see it better.

It's navy blue with a faded patch that's almost pink and a ton of loose threads. There's not a lot to say about it.

I try. "Cool."

Danielle gives me a look that means *Cool? Really?*

The pool is large, with white plastic sunbeds around it. The rest of the group is already in there, swimming, shrieking and abusing the inflatables.

I badly want this to be OK. Stage one: slip into the water speedily so that nobody sees too much of my chub. Stage two: do a couple of strokes of front crawl and feel the water blanket my face.

It will feel good, like it used to.

"Come on!" yells the boy from Cornwall. Joe. He splashes us and Fay shrieks. Danielle takes off her towel and bombs into the water. The lifeguard leans back in his high seat to avoid being splashed and says nothing.

Fay dips a toe in the water and squeaks, "It's freezing!" But she throws her towel on to a sunbed and eases herself, yelping, into the shallow end, elongating herself so she's even thinner. The water reaches midway up her thighs. She looks back at me. "You coming in, Skye?"

"Maybe," I say, but already I can feel my breathing isn't right.

"You can sunbathe later," she says, and squats down into the water with a gasp.

I sit on the end of a sunbed, still wrapped in my towel, and inspect the nail varnish on my toes. They alternate red and pink, a homage to Luisa. It was her signature toe look last summer. Her toes were a lot less ugly than mine.

Somebody's blocking my light. I lift my head and see polo-shirt boy. Brandon. Except he has a bare top half now. He picks up a small beach ball that's under the sunbed nearest to me and catches me looking at him.

"You not swimming?"

Oh, how perceptive. "Nope."

He probably thinks I don't want to get in the water because I'm embarrassed about being seen in a bikini, or because I have my period. I don't care. Either of those things is better than the truth.

four

I shed my towel while no one is looking, lie back and sunbathe behind closed eyes and sunglasses. Fay calls my name from the pool but I ignore her. I hear Joe trying to organize some volleyball-type game. Someone says that without me the teams are uneven. I keep still until it's obvious that the game is under way. Then, because my shoulder feels too hot and I have no suntan lotion, and because the smell of chlorine is making me remember things I don't want to remember, I get to my feet. I'll go back to the room and be the first one ready for the high ropes.

I reach down for my towel, and suddenly I can smell a plant that grew in a pot by the pool at Yew Tree House. It had masses of small white flowers. I spin around, dizzy, desperate to see a bush with small white flowers, to know that I'm not hallucinating a smell. Everything tilts.

I lose my balance and fall. My knee hits and slides across warm, rough stone. It burns with a breath-stopping intensity. When I'm able to, I cry out.

The noise in the pool cuts out immediately.

"Are you OK?" It's one of the boys.

Smooth. I'm in nothing but a bikini and everyone's staring at me. I nod without looking round.

"Oh my God, you're bleeding." That's Fay's voice.

My knee is a mess. I grab my towel and hold it against the blood, so I can't see it any more. Joe is climbing out of the water. He walks over, water bouncing off him on to me before he's even close. "You want me to take a look?" He speaks as if he's a first-aider, like he knows what to do. His board shorts are a swirly pattern of reddish-orange and bright white with a rip on one side. The rip might be part of the design for all I know about surfer chic.

"I'm fine," I say to his anklet. It's a faded green with a little shell woven in. I bet it means something. I bet he has a surfer girlfriend who gave it to him. "It's nothing." With a bit of effort, I stand, slinging the towel across my arm, ignoring my knee.

Now Fay is out of the water. Peering at me, at my knee, medical-student style. "Skye, you should sit on the sunbed for a moment."

The lifeguard is wandering over.

"I'm fine," I say. I slide my feet into my flip-flops and

start hobbling. "It's nothing. I'm heading back to the room. I'll see you later."

Outside the swimming pool enclosure I check my knee. It's scraped rather than deeply cut but it hurts like hell. I rearrange my towel over my shoulders so it doesn't brush against my knee, and limp on past the kitchen area. The double doors are open and I can hear the sound of clanging pans and a high-pressure tap running.

"Skye! Wait up."

I twist round to see Joe run across the grass, barefoot, still wearing only his swim shorts. When he reaches me, he says, "Tell me to get lost if you want, but are you really OK?"

My knee's throbbing, but I don't look down at it. "I'm fine," I say. "Thanks." I have to blink away the threat of tears. I don't know what they're about.

Joe carries on walking beside me. "Don't let it spoil your first day."

I shake my head.

"Look forward, not backwards." He slows his pace. "Easier said than done, I know. I lost Kyra, my girlfriend, last summer."

"Last summer," I begin. *Everything ended and started with last summer.* I suck in enough air to be able to say it: "My sister died."

He smiles. The sympathetic kind. The dead-person-conversation kind. "Summer's a difficult time for both of

23

us, then. What happened to her?"

When I'm ancient, in my nursing home with white hair and a floral nightie that reaches to my toes, I wonder if that question will still make my lungs collapse.

"She ... drowned." *In a pool of red water.*

"How?"

I avoid his eye, and focus on a sign that has one arrow showing the direction of the lake, and another to the campfire area. If I can't say it here, on a BAK-up holiday, maybe I'll never manage to put what happened behind me. Joe isn't an adult who needs to know, or someone who wants the gory details; he's been through the death thing himself. All I need to say is one sentence and ignore the pounding in my chest. "She hit her head as she fell into the pool and was knocked unconscious." I don't know why I add, "There was an argument."

Joe nods. "Sounds traumatic. I hope you weren't there." He sees me hesitate. "Oh, no. You were, weren't you?"

My mouth is dry and my shame a thousand red-hot needles pricking me.

"You couldn't save her?" asks Joe.

He's close to me, peering into my guilty eyes. The towel is making me too hot but I can't take it off. I shake my head.

"No? You poor thing, Skye," says Joe. He touches me lightly on the arm. "I'll let you get back to your room. See you at the high ropes in a bit, yeah? Take it easy."

I watch him jog with long strides back towards the pool.

I should have asked him about Kyra, his lost girlfriend.

My knee is throbbing as I demonstrate to the instructor how I can unclip and clip myself to a wire. Since I'm the last person to do this, I think about doing it wrong, to shake things up a bit. But I'd risk being bumped on to the baby course, where the ropes are half a metre off the ground.

"You have two carabiners on your harness," says the instructor for the gazillionth time. "You must never be on the course without at least one of them being attached to the wire." Her voice is a shouty monotone.

We're all doing this activity, Pippa included. I can tell she's done this before, even though she's making a point of listening ultra-carefully to the instructor.

"No pressuring the people in front of you. Give them space," drones the instructor.

Beside me, Fay has stopped worrying about her helmet, and is now fretting about her harness. It's not tight enough. It's digging into her leg. What if it can't hold her weight?

If it can't hold *her* weight, we're all doomed.

Pippa looks over. "Don't worry. I'll check it in a minute."

Danielle, standing further away, rolls her eyes and scuffs her Vans in the dusty earth.

The instructor says, "Any questions?"

Somebody asks how many accidents have happened.

"I always get asked that," says the instructor in a weary

voice. "The answer is none, and it will stay like that on my watch. You'll be sent home for any stupid or risky behaviour. All righty. Let's queue up." She makes her mouth into a straight line, which is probably as close to a smile as she allows herself to go.

While Pippa checks Fay's harness, I sidle away and merge into the queue to start the course. I end up behind Danielle and in front of Brandon.

We climb a steep ladder to a wooden platform which has a mesh fence round it, apart from the bit where each of us has to step off and swing on a rope a short distance on to some netting. Our instructor stands at the gap, to check each person has clipped on their carabiners.

Joe goes first, leaping in one smooth movement on to the rope netting. "This is awesome!" he shouts as he climbs up to the first proper high ledge.

"Clip on, then go," barks the instructor when it's Danielle's turn. She whoops loudly as she swings.

"Next," says the instructor. I take a deep breath, and as I push off from the platform, my knee seizes up. I try to turn myself so that my other leg will reach the netting first and gain a foothold, but I somehow misjudge it and smash into the netting, my face against it, scrabbling to hold on.

"Smile!" says someone. Above me, on the ledge, Danielle holds her phone in my direction. I glare at her and haul myself up the netting, wincing each time I have to put weight on my bad knee. By the time I reach the ledge, Danielle has long disappeared along a walkway made from swinging wooden steps.

I clip on to the new wire and stop to check out the view for a moment. I see the roof of an accommodation block, a glimpse of a lake with an island in the middle of it, cows in a field. Below are paths, trees and bushes. The drop is brutal, but if I fell the carabiners would save me. Unclipped, I'd be dead for sure.

As I walk along the first plank of wobbly wood, adrenaline pumps through me, deadening the pain in my knee. I'm hyper-aware of everything, from the texture of the rope in my hands to the hardness of the wood beneath my trainers.

For ages, Danielle is well ahead of me, and I'm worried about Brandon catching me up, but then I can't tell if I'm going quicker or she's going slower because I'm closing in on her. I step on to an easy rope-ladder section that she's still on, and she turns to hiss at me, "Give me some space!"

I see straight away that both of her carabiners are lying against her harness, unclipped. If I wobble the walkway too much, she'll lose her footing or fall through a gap. I freeze, breath stuck in my throat, and watch how her hands grip the rope either side of her and her legs tremble as they negotiate each rung. I want to turn away in case I witness something that can never be forgotten, but I can't. I'm here. I know that means I have to see it through, whatever happens. She walks in jerky steps towards the ledge at the end of the section, and I will her to keep going. As soon as both her feet are on it, she clips herself back to the wire with both carabiners and steps on to the next section. She moves lightly now, like a mountain animal. My body is rubbery, weak with delayed fear.

It takes me a long time to catch her up. When I'm close enough, I whisper, "Why did you do that?"

"Do what?" she asks without looking round. "What are you on about?"

five

Yew Tree House, before Nico

I wake in the night because I've had a bad dream about Oscar. He's in hospital again, with Mum, because of an infection, and I dreamed the medicine wasn't working. I know it'll be impossible to go straight back to sleep, so I switch on my bedside light. The chill in the air and extra-quietness make me twitch back the curtain by my bed, and everywhere is white.

Snow. It lies so thickly that you can only tell where the swimming pool starts because of the cover-roller sticking up, but you can't tell where it ends.

It's lonely being the only one in the house who knows about the snow. I hold out for as long as I can, and then

I wrap my duvet round me and walk past Oscar's empty bedroom along the landing to Luisa's room.

"Lu," I say quietly. Sometimes when I stand by her bed at night, she goes mad because for a second she thinks I'm a random crazy who's broken into her room.

Tonight she groans.

"It's snowed!" I sit on her bed. The bed I'm so envious of because it's a double.

"Wow." She sits up, then flops back against her pillows. "I'm too tired to look right now. Go back to bed."

"I can't stop thinking about Oscar."

She sighs. "Get in, but don't put your cold feet anywhere near me. I'm serious."

I leave my duvet on the floor and scoot in beside her. Her bed linen is washed with the same products as mine but it smells different. She goes back to sleep immediately and I snuggle down, gazing at the posters on her wall and planning the snow day ahead.

Loads of people show up on the hill above the farm to slide down on sledges, trays or whatever else they've got available. Toby's there of course, seizing the opportunity to sit on a sledge behind Luisa and cuddle her from behind as they hurtle down the hill. He comes back to the house with us, and volunteers to shovel snow off the doorstep and make a path across the driveway to the gate. No one other than us needs access so I don't get why he does it. The track from the road up to our house and the farm is impassable at the moment. Mum and Oscar are holed up at the hospital and Dad is working from home at the top of the house in his office.

Toby slurps hot chocolate with us in the kitchen afterwards, and when Luisa says she has to finish off an essay, he points at the back garden and says incredulously, "What? When there's all that fresh snow?"

"I need to get good grades if I want to go to uni," she says. "Make a snowman with Skye."

We do. We make the sort that's standing on its head, we jump on the trampoline, which hardly bounces because of the weight of the snow on it, and we make snow angels. We have a snowball fight that ends when Toby shakes a tree branch above my head and I'm snow-dumped so badly I can barely stay upright, and neither can he because he finds it so hilarious.

"Don't you have to help in the farm shop or something?" I ask as I trudge inside. He toes off his boots and follows me in to say goodbye to Luisa, dripping water up the stairs. As I remove my sodden outer layers in the kitchen, he shouts down to me that she's not doing her essay at all, she's watching a film on her laptop. I walk into her room, and he's in bed with her, stripped down to his T-shirt, already sucked into the drama on screen.

Luisa looks up, sees my damp hair and red ears and hands, and says, "Are you OK?"

"I'm frozen."

"Get a hot-water bottle and another duvet, and watch this with us."

Before the film finishes, I fall asleep, huddled on my side away from the other two. I wake up slowly, warm and comfortable, listening to their conversation.

"I don't think Dad meant to tell me, but he'd had a few drinks," Luisa is saying. "They've spent so much money seeing doctors abroad, his business isn't doing well at the moment and Mum can't work any more because of Oscar."

I open my eyes, eyelashes scratching on the pillow.

Toby shifts. I can tell he's not leaning against Luisa any more. "Your parents wouldn't sell this house though. . . . I mean, you've lived here all your life. And. . ."

"Don't worry. I'll sell a kidney to help them out," says Luisa in a jokey, upbeat voice.

"I'd sell a kidney if it meant you staying here," says Toby. "I'd sell my body."

Luisa laughs, and next there's the off-putting sound of noisy kissing.

six

Now

"How did everyone find the high ropes course?" asks Pippa as we line up for pasta bake and salad in the yellow dining room.

Everyone mutters that they had a good time apart from Fay, who yaps on about the parts she hated, which is most of it, and Danielle, who plays on her phone.

When I reach the food, I scoop up some pasta with the serving spoon and tap it against my plate until it falls off in one solid block. I decorate it round the edge with salad leaves.

"There are sauces at the end," says Pippa. "I can recommend the sweet chilli."

I shuffle along behind the others towards the jars and

bottles. There's mustard, ketchup, lots of different salad dressings, barbecue sauce and a jar of Lower Road Farm Sweet Chilli Sauce. I place my plate on the table and pick up the chilli sauce. The label with the curly font is hauntingly familiar. A waft of the sweet red sauce is all it takes to transport me back to the farm shop. I see an open tester jar on a table in the middle of the shop, fragments of savoury crackers on a white plate for dipping. I must have taken a step backwards, because I bump into one of the girls, who I think is called Kerry. Salad drops on to the floor from her plate.

"Watch out!"

Other people stream past me.

"Give it a try," says Pippa, next to me now. "It's made by a local family and sold through their farm shop in a village called Pitford. I've started going there myself."

I know the family. We used to live next door.

When I was offered this holiday, I knew Morley Hill was about half an hour away by car from Pitford, and that seemed an OK distance. Near enough to feel closer to my old life, but far enough away not to be confronted by it. Now I'm not so sure. I touch the neck of the jar with my finger and bring it to my tongue, and let the fresh fiery taste scorch my taste buds.

"The centre likes to order food from local suppliers where possible," carries on Pippa.

I picture the bottles of chilli sauce on the shelving near the door of the farm shop, with the pickles and olives. "Is there a boy about nineteen who works there?"

Pippa looks surprised. "Yes. D'you know the shop?"

So Toby still works there. I haven't seen him for a long time, barely thought about him. He's part of my life that I've shut off.

"I know the area a bit," I say in a way that I hope makes her think we've had holidays round here. I pool a tiny amount of sauce on the side of my plate and look for a spare seat. One that's not too near Fay.

After we've eaten, Pippa stands up to announce there's going to be an evening campfire. With singing. She genuinely thinks that singing is going to sell it to us. Then she remembers the other details: "And a proper fire." Lucky us. With groups of younger kids, Pippa tells us, they have to use red and orange light bulbs. The only parts that sound remotely worthwhile are the hot chocolate on arrival, and marshmallows to roast on the fire.

This is the reason I arrive early in the small clearing, on the edge of Morley Hill land. Fay is with me, even though she hadn't had time to tie her hair up before we left our room, and is doing it now. Her hair elastic has little plastic cupcakes hanging from it.

The hot chocolate tastes watery, and there's not an aerosol of cream in sight, but the marshmallows, eaten off sticks, are good. Fay says she doesn't eat them because they contain gelatin, but she takes one anyway and pulls it apart, dropping the tiny pieces in the fire and licking her fingers afterwards.

We sit on logs with spiky slivers of wood sticking out of them. They're far more of a health and safety risk than the small fire. We must be close to a farm because I can smell it, and even at this time in the evening there's the faint rumble of what might be a tractor or forklift truck.

At the end of primary school, I wrote in the yearbook that my ambition was to be a farmer. I hung out at Lower Road Farm whenever I could. I loved the Mulligan family, the farm dogs and having the freedom to roam. My perfect day was swimming followed by helping at the farm shop. Sometimes when both Mum and Dad took Oscar to see the heart doctor in Germany, Luisa and I slept in the twin beds in the tiny spare bedroom in the farmhouse, and I'd pretend that we were Mulligans, not Coltons.

"I'm looking forward to the singing," says Fay.

"Seriously?" I say. Fay and I have *nothing* in common.

"I've done singing exams," says Fay. "Quite a few of them."

"You'll have to get mingling with the Red group," I say as I throw a dry twig into the fire. It explodes with a mini bang.

I lean down to forage for more twigs and Pippa announces that as everyone's arrived, she's going to pass a clipboard round for us to select what activity we want to do in the morning. And song sheets. Laminated. If I chucked mine in the fire, there would probably be interesting coloured smoke, and dripping words.

Pippa divides us into two groups and tries to get us to do a song with one group coming in after the other. We mumble along self-consciously, but the group that doesn't have Pippa singing with them (mine) flounders. I worry it's only a matter of time before she introduces some actions.

Instead of actions, we get a bearded guy and his guitar joining us. Pippa introduces him as if he's some indie hotshot taking a break in his touring schedule, and settles him down on a log. He starts up with some twangy folksy number and without meaning to I catch Danielle's eye across the fire. The smoke curls in front of her body but I can see she's signalling something to me. She gets up from her log and melts away into the fading evening light, and I stand up to do the same.

Next to me, as if she's attached by string, Fay tugs on the bottom of my fleece. "Where are you going?"

The toilet is the obvious answer, but Fay would probably decide she needed to go too. "To get my jacket. I'm a bit cold," I hiss. "Back in a minute." I disappear before Fay can offer me any of her garments. Not that they'd fit me.

I follow the direction Danielle went in, back towards our accommodation block, before I hear her say in a low voice, "Over here."

After a couple of seconds I see her. She's not that far from the path, under a tree, merging with the shadows. As I walk over, I see she has a lit cigarette in her hand. With a controlled breath she releases the smoke from her mouth.

Wordlessly, she offers me a cigarette from a half-full packet of twenty.

"What were you doing on the high ropes?" I say as I take one.

"I wanted to see what it would feel like."

"I might have had to watch you die."

"True," says Danielle. "But I didn't die and you got an extra shot of adrenaline, so we're both happy, right?"

I place the cigarette on my lips. This will be my second ever cigarette. When I was in the swim squad, I was obsessed with protecting my lungs from pollution. I held my breath when I passed someone in the street who was smoking. I deliberately avoided trafficky roads if I was walking or cycling. Anyone would have thought it was me who was sickly, not my brother.

Danielle eases a lighter from her jeans pocket and holds the flame so that I have to lean towards her. I suck in, and breathe out tar-tainted breath.

"That was pathetic, wasn't it?" says Danielle. I think she's talking about my smoking technique until she jerks her head towards the campfire.

My first cigarette was a couple of months ago, at a party, with a boy whose name I've forgotten. It was the first party I'd been to since moving near London. I wasn't sure why I'd been invited. Or why I'd gone. We sat on the wall outside the house, and it felt similar to now. Being apart from the crowd, and from the music. There were probably a few police or ambulance sirens in the distance though. Here it's country-quiet. No car sounds but plenty of creaking, rustling ones.

"What's your story, then?" asks Danielle.

I let nicotine surge into my lungs before I reply. "Dead sister."

Danielle nods and drops her fag end, grinding it into the patchy earth with her flip-flop. "How old was she?"

"Eighteen."

"How'd it happen – disease, accident, murder?"

"I don't like talking about it," I say.

"Oh," says Danielle. "OK." She's lighting another cigarette for herself. "My golden ticket to this holiday camp is a dead mum. She was forty-four. So you get more tragedy points."

"I'm sorry about your mum," I say.

"It was cancer," says Danielle. She turns away to breathe out her smoke. "By the way, you've got to see the video I took of you face-planting against that net this afternoon."

She produces her phone and scrolls through to find it. "Here."

"It's not that funny," I say, watching myself splat against the rope mesh. The harness makes me look as if I'm wearing one of those contraptions that babies bounce in.

Danielle snatches her phone back. "I might upload it on to this webpage I know. People vote for the best ones." She bats away any questions by waving her arm. "It's just for a laugh. I won't tag you."

I flick the ash off my cigarette. It flutters towards the

ground, scatters and vanishes. "What if I don't give you permission?"

"Come on," says Danielle. "With that helmet, your face is mostly hidden, and it's hardly revenge porn."

"What if I'd filmed you while you weren't clipped on?"

She smiles. "I'd have been impressed. Hey, watch this." She blows a series of smoke rings that rise up into the air, delicate and precise, like some kind of signal.

Luisa took up smoking at university but I only knew because I saw a packet in her open bag last summer. We were in a café in Hoathley and I was minding her bag on my lap while she bought milkshakes, her treat. Mine was Oreo cookie and fudge flavour. I'd spent ages choosing it, but I couldn't finish it. My stomach was smaller then.

"I found your cigarettes," I told her with a stern expression when she brought the milkshakes over.

Anger flared in her face, and she put the drinks down so abruptly hers spilled over the edge. "Did you go through my bag?" She snatched it from me. "What's in there is my business."

"You left your bag open and I saw them," I said. "I didn't touch anything. Honest."

Her face softened. "It's all right. It doesn't matter, but don't do it again."

"OK. But I don't think you should be smoking. Just saying." It didn't occur to me that she might be carrying round other stuff in her bag. Illegal stuff with a high street value.

seven

Thuds, shouts and screams, and I'm running. I'm on a treadmill and I can't reach the swimming pool. Eventually I run faster than the treadmill and I dive into the water. Although I can see Luisa, she's far away, at the bottom of the unfeasibly deep pool. She waves to me. My lungs struggle but I reach her and pull her up by her arms. With swelling panic, I see the brightness of the surface, but I don't think I can make it. The water swirls and I can no longer breathe. I'm suffocating. And then the full unspeakable horror dawns on me. I've let go. I've let Luisa slip away.

I wake, gasping for air, heart exploding, my entire body damp with sweat. It's not the worst of the recurring nightmares. The worst is the one where I manage to rescue Luisa. From water or a fire or a crashed car. I shout at her to wake up, over and over, and she opens her eyes. For an exquisite moment I'm happy. Until she spits blood at me, screaming that I'm a coward and she'll never forgive me. Her eyes roll back in her head and her body disintegrates in my arms.

For several seconds I stay utterly still, unsure if I was screaming or crying in my sleep. There's no movement from the other two, only steady breathing. If I close my eyes now, I'll get the flashbacks. To the changing room, the red water, Luisa's lifeless body. I wait it out, one hand on my stomach, feeling my breaths go in and out until I'm steady again, and fatigue creeps through my brain.

When I wake up later, I'm not sure where I am. It's disorienting but not unpleasant. It's as if for those brief seconds I might have slipped into someone else's life, with all their possibilities and opportunities. Bright light filters through the orange curtains, and makes a criss-cross pattern on the bottom half of Fay's duvet cover.

I reach for my phone, see that Mum's already texted me twice, and skim through my social media sites. Once, I'd have woken to messages from my best friend, Annika, and the others. Maybe from Max Tomkins too. That was when swim squad was pretty much the whole of my life, and Annika and I were training for the same dream – to swim at nationals.

Sometimes I'd have messages from Luisa, often sent to our own private chat group via the MessageHound app, a link to something she thought I'd like or a photo. Today the only message I have from someone other than Mum is from a girl in my English class asking what book we're supposed to be reading over the summer.

Breakfast is in the main dining room, which is its own separate chalet building, and the place is swarming with teenagers. I've left Fay and Danielle in bed – they say they'd rather miss breakfast and have a longer lie-in. At least Danielle does, and I've worked out that Fay isn't much of an eater. I queue up by myself for a selection of buffet food, and assemble a bacon and egg croissant sandwich at an empty table.

"Oh dear. Are you all on your own?" Joe's standing on the other side of the table with a tray of fruit, yoghurt and juice. He's wearing palm-tree-patterned board shorts and a tight black-and-white rash vest.

"Yep," I say. "But I don't mind."

He sits opposite me and takes a swig of his orange juice. "So, how are you finding things?" he asks, as if he's just got himself a counselling qualification.

"OK," I say, and bite into my deluxe croissant.

"That's good. You know, if you want to talk about anything, I'm right here."

I think he's expecting me to thank him, but I nod and check that no one is listening in to this excruciating conversation. On the next table a group of Reds are arguing over who broke a music stand the day before.

Joe stirs his yoghurt. "Guilt is very challenging."

I shouldn't have told him what happened to Luisa. I can't believe I was so stupid. "Please. Don't."

"Oh. OK." He looks surprised. "I thought you didn't want me to tell anyone, not that you weren't happy to talk about it with me." He swallows down a large spoonful of yogurt. "By the way, I can be trusted completely not to tell anyone."

I take another bite of my croissant, and eat more quickly. I want breakfast to be over.

"Did you choose kayaking or archery for this morning's activity?" asks Joe.

"Kayaking." I ticked it because of what happened at the pool yesterday. I want to get over my water phobia. To be braver. The kayaking lake won't be the same as the swimming pool. It won't smell of chlorine, I'll be wearing a life jacket and I'm going to be in a boat. Nothing like the swimming pool, in fact, but it's a first step.

"Are you much of a kayaker?" he asks. His eyebrows tell me he doubts it.

"No," I say. I've never actually been in a kayak.

"You've got to have stamina for kayaking," says Joe.

Stamina was something the old me used to have. In the days when fifty lengths of the Hoathley pool was only the warm-up at training. "I'm sure I'll be OK," I say.

"I can keep an eye on you," says Joe. "I've kayaked on rivers, in the sea, in rapids. . . I know my stuff."

I take hold of my tray and stand up. "Thanks," I say. "Good to know." Who does he think he is – my dad?

Danielle doesn't want to do anything. She wants to stay in the room and sleep some more. Fay, naturally, has chosen the same activity as me.

As we follow the signposts to the boathouse, she lists her kayaking worries. What if she can't keep up with the group, her hair goes uncontrollably frizzy, or she falls out of the kayak and gets trapped underneath it without enough oxygen?

"You should stick with Joe," I say. "He told me at breakfast he's an expert."

"You sat with Joe?" says Fay. "What did you talk about?"

"Kayaking," I say. She might as well have *I Fancy Joe* printed on her crop top.

The lake is huge with its own little jungle island in the middle, covered in trees. It's surrounded by the woods where the high-ropes course is – I can see a few of the really tall wooden posts sticking up above the treeline. It's peaceful here, though probably less so once people get going on the high-ropes course and the screaming starts.

We make our way to the boathouse, which is a long, rickety building. Two huge wooden doors facing the lake are wide open and reveal rows and rows of kayaks inside, slotted into their compartments like wine bottles in a rack. The grassy area in front of the building slopes gently down to the water and a wooden jetty. There are two benches on the grass and a sign by the jetty: *No fishing. No swimming. No trespassing on island (nature reserve).*

"I'd like to live on an island like that," says Fay. "All on my own. Far away from everyone."

Fay is the least likely person to cope with living on an island on her own, but I let that pass.

Joe's already standing outside the boathouse with the kayaking instructor. The two of them are deep in conversation about sprints, marathons and personal bests. Tacked to one of the doors is a list of participants for this morning's session. I see we're waiting for three more people. Kerry, Alice and Brandon.

They arrive together, and the instructor comes over to see if Brandon wants to borrow a T-shirt from lost property to avoid ruining his shirt.

Brandon glances down at his geometric print shirt, creased in rectangles as if it's fresh out of a packet, and shakes his head. "I'm good, thanks." He rolls up his sleeves to the elbow as we follow Tim, the instructor, into the gloomy boathouse through a side door. We leave everything we don't want to get soaked or lost overboard in wire cubes, and clip ourselves into damp life jackets.

Tim gives us paddles, which we wave around on dry land to get an idea of the technique. He stands with his back to the lake so that we face it as we copy his movements. I avoid looking at the water, which is waiting for me, murky and unappealing.

The boats are longer and heavier than I was expecting, with dank water swilling about at the bottom. We carry them down to the jetty, where Tim says he'll hold each person's boat while they get in, apart from Joe's, who knows what he's doing.

Joe goes first. Fay volunteers to go next, probably so that she can be alone on the lake with Joe for a few minutes. She does a bit of shrieking as she paddles away from the jetty, but she seems to be able to make the kayak go wherever she wants.

Kerry goes next, followed by Alice, then it's my turn.

"Good luck," says Brandon.

I glare at him because he didn't say that to the others. Does he think I'm totally hopeless?

My bare feet make uneasy contact with the old lake water in the boat, and I thump down on the seat sooner than I'm expecting. As soon as I dip the paddle into the water on one side, I feel the whole thing tip, my stomach sliding with it. I shift my body so it's more centred.

"Feeling good, Skye?" yells Joe. He couldn't sound more patronizing if he tried.

I nod but don't give him the satisfaction of eye contact. I move the paddle how we were shown on the bank but I'm finding it hard to look at the water and not see a red tint to it. There's a lump of panic in my throat. I think about the breathing lessons I had from the counsellor at school. *Breathe in slowly through your nose for a count of five. Imagine your lungs are a bottle and you're filling it with air from the bottom up. Hold for three. Breathe out through your mouth for a count of five.*

It helps a bit.

Everyone's in their boat now. Tim calls us over to him. He's going to lead us round the lake. We'll go at a gentle pace. It's going to be fun. The perfect way to spend a sunny morning. He can't believe he gets paid for this.

Kerry and Alice want to go behind Tim; Fay angles herself next to Joe. I hang back, and I find myself alongside Brandon.

"Having fun?" he asks.

"Bucketloads," I say. "How about you?"

He slices the paddle through the water at the wrong angle and water sprays him. "Should have chosen archery. Some of the lake water just went in my mouth. D'you think I'll get sick?" He lets his boat glide and peers at the water. "I bet there's all kinds of poisonous algae in there. Can't you die from some water-rat disease?" His face wrinkles up in disgust.

"Possibly," I say. "You're such a townie."

"Oi. You live in London too."

"*Near*," I say. "And I haven't always lived there." I shove my paddle in the water. "Come on. We'd better catch up with the others."

As we move closer to the island, I see that although it's mostly thickly forested, it has a pebbly beach all round it. Like a desert island without the sand or palm trees. Without me noticing, my kayak has drifted away from the group and I need to go more to the right, but I've lost the rhythm of my paddle... I push it too far into the water with too much of my body weight behind it. My legs are crossed and I can't right myself in time. *No.* I can't fall in. I can't. *Please no.*

I fall. The water is freezing. A shock. In the half second that my head is underwater, all the nightmares I've had about drowning resurface in my head. Icy fear grips me. The desperate desire to breathe, the chest pain and the panic. As I tread water and keep my head up, I think of blood leaking into water, drifting in red clouds.

Breathe.

I'm wearing a life jacket. If I need to I can flip on to my back. I'm not that far from the shore. I can swim.

I'm aware of boats near me, voices that sharpen into sense.

Joe's voice: "I'll get her kayak."

Fay's: "Skye! Skye?"

Tim's: "Skye, you'll be able to put your feet down in a minute."

My feet find the gravelly bottom of the lake. Tim is there beside me in his boat. "Nice swim? We'll get you back in your boat in no time." He shouts to Joe. "Hey, mate. Bring her kayak over."

I walk through the thigh-high water in slow motion. "I'm not going back out," I say. "I've had enough."

"Hey, don't be embarrassed," says Tim. "It's a sunny day – you'll soon dry off."

"I'm not going back out," I repeat. "You can't make me."

"Go on. Be brave," says Tim.

Be brave.

I keep wading.

Tim shouts at the others. "I won't be a mo." He clambers out of his boat into the water, not even registering the coldness of it. "I'll help you on to dry land."

He grabs the back of my life jacket and hauls me forward on to the jetty like I'm an enormous dead fish. I crawl on to my knees, then stagger to my feet.

"I'll sort out your boat," says Tim. "You go to the boathouse. There's a towel on the back of the door. OK?"

I nod, then shiver up the slope towards the boathouse. I wish that he'd stood on the jetty with me for a moment and put his arms round me. I know he wouldn't have been allowed to. Child protection issues and all that. But for the first time in a year I want someone to hug me, and tell me they know how hard it was for me to be in the water.

The towel on the back of the boathouse door smells of wet dog but it's dry. I take off my life jacket, wrap the towel round me, over my wet T-shirt and shorts, and grab my flip-flops from the rack. As I squelch out of the boathouse, I see Brandon lugging his kayak up the slope.

"What's the matter?" I ask.

"I wanted to check you were OK."

"No, seriously."

He gives a mini shrug. "Had enough of the lake tour. Wasn't my thing." He unclips the fastening on the front of his life jacket and lets it hang open. "But you are OK?"

I nod. All this checking-I'm-OK business is wearying,

He dumps the boat down and contemplates the mud between his toes. "I'd better go back for a shower." But he plonks himself on a bench and sighs.

I sit down on the other one and curl my knees up. I'm reminded of sitting with Annika by the side of a pool. Huddled under a towel, though usually it smelled a lot more pleasant. Exhausted, with no energy to move.

After people started to hear about what happened, Annika came round and gave me a present. A cutesy little teddy on a key ring wearing an obscene pair of red Speedos. It was the sort of thing that used to make me laugh, but it went in a box for the charity shop when we moved. Every time I looked at it, I was reminded of Annika crying, and me not able to say a single word.

I miss Annika.

The others are on the far side of the island now. Blocked from view.

"You freaked me out when you first fell in," says Brandon.

"Why? Were you worried I'd swallowed some water?"

"I could see you were panicking. Can you swim? Did you lie on that form we had to fill in?"

I give him a look that means *You what*? "I'm a club swimmer," I say, before I correct myself. "*Was* a club swimmer. I've swum in south of England competitions. I've got trophies and everything."

"Then why were you acting so weirdly?" asks Brandon. Why does everyone have to be so nosy?

"Bad memories," I say. I stand up. Make sure my feet are firmly in my flip-flops, so I'm not going to slip. "See you later. I'm off to have a shower."

eight

I'm the first person in the yellow dining room for lunch. Danielle's second. She tells me she was hoicked out of our room by Pippa after Fay and I left for the lake this morning. Apparently, staying in bed wasn't on the list of this morning's options, but she was allowed to sunbathe on the patio outside the games room.

"How was kayaking?" she asks as she takes the food wrap off a basket of garlic bread and takes a chunk.

I help myself to one too.

Danielle keeps going even though her mouth is full. "Your hair's wet. Did you fall in?"

"I had a shower." Not technically a lie.

A member of the catering staff bustles in and grabs at the food wrap covering the other bowls, as if she's being timed. The archery crowd come through the door with Pippa, and I take a plate from the pile and get moving.

The kayakers don't turn up until I've almost finished my first course. They drib-drab in, Joe and Fay ahead of Kerry and Alice.

"Look at that," says Danielle. "Someone is actually listening to Fay."

Fay's standing close to Joe. Her face is tilted up towards his and she's telling him some long, involved story. Joe is nodding and smiling.

"She's not his type," I say.

"How d'you know what someone's type is?" says Danielle.

I shrug, and fork some coleslaw into my mouth. "The two of them don't . . . match. I can't explain it."

"That's stereotyping," says Danielle. "You're saying that people need to match? What, like in skin colour or level of attractiveness?"

"Course not," I say, as I watch Fay and Joe leave the buffet table and head for the two spare seats next to me.

"It's cute," says Danielle. "They're both as annoying as each other."

I brace myself for the conversation that's about to take place just as soon as Joe and Fay reach me.

"Skye!" calls Fay, before there's a sensible talking distance between us. "Are you all right? Did you swallow any lake water?"

Danielle thumps her fists on the table with delight. "Oh. My. God. You *did*. You fell in!"

54

Fay takes the place next to me, and Joe sits the other side of her. "How are you?" he asks, leaning forward to hear my answer.

"Fine," I say. "Yeah, fine."

Joe tells me how I missed a great paddle round the lake. "You *and* him," he says, nodding towards the door, as Brandon walks into the dining room. He's changed into clean shorts and a green polo shirt. I'm grateful there are no more spare seats on our table. The sooner we can get this discussion over with, with the least amount of people, the better.

"You should have got back in the boat," says Joe. "You know, like getting back on a horse. Without fear there is no courage."

I roll my eyes. "Spare me the inspirational quotes."

Danielle laughs. "I wish I'd gone kayaking now. I could have filmed you falling in."

Joe holds his hand up, palm out. "That's bullying."

He has a point.

"Lighten up," says Danielle.

"If you knew what happened with my girlfriend you wouldn't say that," says Joe.

"What happened?" asks Fay. She rests her fork on the side of her plate

"Cyberbullying." He pours some water into his glass. "Which led to suicide." It's weird the way he says it. As if he's delivering an important line in a play.

"That's awful," Fay murmurs.

"Yes," says Joe. "It's been a nightmare."

55

Fay bites her lower lip.

"What sort of cyberbullying?" asks Danielle.

"There was a photo... It got circulated."

"A sexting thing?" asks Danielle.

"Kyra took a naked selfie and..." He leans back and runs both hands through each side of his blond surfer hair. I'm embarrassed for him. "The police were involved," he says. "There was an enquiry. But nothing happened."

"So nobody got the blame?" asks Fay.

Joe shakes his head. "Kyra went to a different school to me. I tried to find out if anyone got expelled or anything, but no one would tell me." He sounds bitter.

There's a pause. All of us are used to The Pause. It's the one where other people leap in and say, "I'm so sorry." Then they usually don't know what to say next.

Fay gets there first. "I'm so sorry, Joe."

Danielle says, "It pisses me off that people don't know the difference between banter and bullying."

I want to get up and leave. I don't want to hear Joe's sad story aired and flapped about. But we have to wait around for Pippa's after-lunch chat, so while I squish crumbs of carrot cake on to my finger and eat them, one by one, I listen to more details, responses to questions from Fay and Danielle. Kyra was found in the garden shed by her mum. She'd taken a fatal overdose of her granddad's pain relief medication. Joe found out from a friend.

He tells us how gorgeous Kyra was. Later, when he has his phone, he'll show us some photos. She was a surfer.

That's how they met. She gave him his anklet a couple of weeks before she died. He hasn't taken it off since.

So I was right about that anklet.

The afternoon's activities are Ultimate Frisbee or orienteering, followed by a workshop called Coping with Difficult Feelings, then a table football tournament. None of it is compulsory but Pippa is keen for people to Have Fun, and Make the Most of What's on Offer. She has a further announcement.

"Today is Brandon's sixteenth birthday."

She waits for the cheering to calm down, and I search him out. He's on the other table. Squirming. I can't believe he didn't mention it this morning. He's had a pretty crap birthday so far. A tiny bit of kayaking which he didn't enjoy. Me walking away from him in a huff.

"He doesn't want a fuss," says Pippa. "But we couldn't let the occasion go past unnoticed, so there'll be a cake in here at four-thirty p.m."

Someone starts clapping, Danielle whoops and Brandon does a mock bow in his seat as acknowledgement but looks embarrassed.

"What activity are you choosing?" Fay asks Joe.

"Frisbee," says Joe. "How about you?"

"Same," says Fay.

How very unsurprising. But it's helped me make my mind up — orienteering it is.

*

Only three Yellows want to do orienteering: me, Danielle and Brandon.

"Are you sure you're not stalking me?" I ask him, but in a nicer way than if I didn't know it was his birthday.

As this is an inter-group activity, we're waiting by the stone steps outside the main dining room for Blues and Reds to join us. Brandon says, "Are you sure you're not stalking *me*? I'm pretty sure I put up my hand before you did." He adds, "But I'm OK with you stalking me."

I shrug. "Happy birthday, by the way."

"Cheers."

Danielle looks up from where she's been watching loads of ants crawl in and out of a crack in the cement below the bottom step. "I'm not feeling this orienteering thing any more. I need a cigarette."

Two girls wander up. "Is this where we're supposed to wait for orienteering?"

"Yeah," I say.

"Are you the music lot?" asks the same girl. She has incredibly long hair, blonde and very straight.

"Nope," says Danielle.

"Are you *Yellows*?" asks the other girl. She sounds quite excited. "Here with the charity?"

I nod.

"I hope you don't mind me asking," says the girl who looks like Rapunzel, "but do you all have . . . I don't know how to put this . . . mental health issues?"

We stare at her.

"I don't mean to be funny, but we heard that you had therapy sessions."

"It's a bereavement charity," says Danielle.

Rapunzel looks blank.

"We have issues with death," says Danielle.

"What?" says the other girl. She looks at her friend, confused.

"My nan died on her own birthday," says Rapunzel. "My dad had to take her present back to the shops."

"Thanks for sharing," says Danielle. "Have you seen how many ants there are here? There must be a nest."

"Eugh," says Rapunzel. "That's gross." She and her friend edge away, while the three of us ant-watch in silence.

Soon there are fifteen of us and an instructor in a red T-shirt. As we have to divide into groups of three, our group comes ready formed.

"Why did we get here so early?" moans Danielle, as the instructor has to placate a leftover Red who isn't happy to be teamed up with the two remaining Blues.

Eventually, we're given a map, compass, pen and a folded-over sheet of paper printed with instructions and a quiz. The instructor says we have to stay within the activity centre grounds, which includes some farmland that's rented from Morley Hill. We mustn't trample any crops or annoy any livestock or farmers.

There's a five-minute lag between each group setting off. We're last, which means by the time we set off,

Danielle definitely isn't feeling the orienteering any more. As we walk within sight of our accommodation block, she peels off and says she'll see us for cake. She dumps the pen and scrumpled quiz in Brandon's hands.

I'd like to peel off too, and go and sunbathe somewhere, but it's Brandon's birthday and I can't leave him on his own. We walk on in silence, past the mini go-karting track and towards the campfire area. There's no sign of any of the other orienteering groups.

"Would you rather have the compass and map?" I ask. "I only took them because I'm OK with coordinates and map stuff."

"Whatever you want," he says, stopping at a fork in the path. "I don't mind."

I come to a halt next to him and check the map. "This way." I point towards the left-hand path, and we walk on in more silence. "Listen. I don't mind finding short cuts if you want to get back quicker. We don't have to bother with the quiz either." I stop. "We don't have to do *any* of it. It's your birthday – your call."

Brandon appears defeated by all the options I've given him. "I don't know," he says. "Let's get away from here for a bit."

"All right." I remember seeing a locked five-bar gate near the campfire area. The other side of it was a field of wheat. "I know a good escape route."

When the gate's a few metres away, I demonstrate my five-bar-gate vault, including run-up. Brandon gives it a go but screws it up. He lands on the other side of the gate in a heap.

I can't help laughing. I haven't laughed for such a long time. Not out loud.

Brandon stands up and brushes off the dusty earth. "Thanks for asking if I'm OK."

"You can't be grumpy on your birthday."

"I can."

"I'll have to do my impression of a pigeon. It used to make my family laugh."

Brandon says, "Go on then."

It's not that funny, and I'm out of practice. I stutter my neck, strut about and roll my Rs to create a curled-up cooing noise.

He doesn't laugh, but he smiles. "Interesting talent."

"Consider it a birthday present."

"Lucky me," say Brandon. He says it with sarcasm, but not the sharp-edged type.

There's a footpath along the edge of the field. We climb over a stile, on to a narrow road that's more like a tunnel because some of the trees either side have branches that almost meet in the middle. There's a footpath sign pointing down the road, but Brandon jerks his head towards a field of cows.

"Let's go cross-country," he says.

"You're not scared of cows?"

He frowns. "No. Should I be?"

"Nope, but let's walk round them."

I follow him over the gate. No vaults this time – I've done enough showing off. We go towards the top end of the field, up near a stone wall. There's a large modern house the other side with a massive climbing frame in the garden. As we go closer, we hear the sounds of people – a family, probably – eating outside, talking, laughing, clinking cutlery and plates about. I see the top of a sunshade at the side of the house.

Brandon flops with his back against the stone wall. I think he's about to get his phone out and take a photo of the cows, but he just stares down the field at them. "Want to hear my cow impression?"

"OK."

"Get ready. This is going to be good." He opens his mouth and makes a loud, bellowing *moooo* sound. The family stop making quite so much noise. Brandon moos again, even louder.

"What *is* that?" we hear someone say.

Another moo, but this one is less convincing because Brandon is laughing. I'm laughing too. Birds fly up from the trees in the lane behind us, and we sense that some of the family are no longer at the table, and are walking towards the wall.

Brandon touches my arm and indicates that we'd better go. We start running.

nine

We run towards a thick clump of trees at the edge of the field. It's the most obvious place to run to so there's no discussion. It just makes sense. Some of the cows run too, after us, which makes Brandon scream. When we reach the gate to the wooded area, we hurdle over it and for a few seconds all we can do is gasp as much oxygen into our lungs as we can. After I've studied the map, I tell him that we can go one more field over and join a road that will take us through the village back to the activity centre. My heart's returned to its usual rate but I'm feeling pumped up. Alive.

Brandon's still too puffed to talk but he nods.

We walk through the trees, and out into another wheat

field and sunshine. I look ahead for a gap in the thick hedgerow so we can squeeze through.

"No cows, that's good," says Brandon. "Let's stop for a moment."

"Here?"

"Yeah. I've got a stitch." He sits down in a shadowy patch of thin grass, and I settle myself down too, a little apart from him, as if we're about to lay out food for a picnic. I really wish we had a cool bag full of drinks.

"Knackered and thirsty in a field in the middle of nowhere. Not how you thought you'd be spending your birthday, then," I say.

"I don't mind," he says.

"Seriously? You wouldn't rather be with your family or your friends?"

All I know about Brandon is that he lives in London – which could mean relatively near my house or ages away by car or public transport – and that his mum made him go on this holiday. And that he likes designer shirts.

"To be honest, it would make me miss my brother more."

"He's why you're here?" Code for *Your brother's dead?*

"Yeah. He was a couple of years older than me. You?"

"My sister. Four years older than me, but. . ."

"You were close?"

I nod.

"Are you parents still together?"

I was expecting the how-did-it-happen question, not

that. "Yes." Some days, though, they can't talk to each other or they snap, both grey with exhaustion, worry and sadness.

"Mine divorced," says Brandon. "They told me my dad's work had asked him to go to the States but it was obvious he'd asked for a transfer. He couldn't hack it at home any more."

I pick the grass in front of me, and make a little pile of it.

"They did so much lying, my parents," says Brandon. "They lied to my brother. Told him that the doctors thought there was still a chance he'd get better. They told me not to worry, that everything would work out OK when they knew it wouldn't. There's a difference between hoping and lying. They lied."

"I guess they thought they were doing the right thing," I say.

"My mum hooked up with this guy soon after." He has a slow, clear way of talking, as if he might be reading an autocue. "A white guy this time. Like her. My dad and my brother got airbrushed out of history." He pauses, and I wait. I know not to jump in with my big feet. Too many people have done it to me this past year. "So they had a baby, yeah. My sister. Half-sister. She's white too." He pauses. "So now I'm the only black kid – the only black *person* – in my family. It happened fast."

I feel different from the rest of my family too. I just don't know how to say it in words.

"It used to be my mum who looked like the odd one out," says Brandon. "Now it's me."

"Why did she make you come on this holiday?"

He rolls his eyes. "She says I'm angry. Oh, and I'm failing my brother by not working hard enough at school – how does she work that one out?" He looks at me. "Sorry, I've gone on too much. Tell me about you and your sister."

Brandon's easier to talk to than I thought, but I'm not about to make the same mistake with him as I did with Joe. Everything's simpler when people don't know too much about me and Luisa, whoever they are. "You don't want to be depressed on your birthday."

"It's all right. I've postponed it until I'm home." He blows at the grass cuttings in front of me, so they disappear, as if he's blowing out candles on a cake. "Anyway, this bit of my birthday's not bad. You know, sitting in a field with you." He gives me a lopsided smile. I can't tell if he's making a joke.

"Yeah. Londoners don't often get to sit in fields. Exciting," I say.

We look round us. At the pale crop, the blue sky and the drifting clouds. The gap between the two of us seems smaller. Touching distance. I stand up and say, "Let's do a wheat angel. Like a snow angel."

He's no idea what I'm talking about.

"You've never done a snow angel? It's what you do when it snows." I push away the memory of doing snow angels with Toby in the garden of Yew Tree House, of feeling safe in bed with Luisa.

He shakes his head.

"You lie on the ground and move your arms up and down to make wings, and shift your legs from side to side for the long skirty bit." I dump the map and compass on the ground and wade out into the field. "I don't know if it will work with wheat but we should try it. Come on."

Brandon chucks the pen next to the map and compass, folds up the quiz and pushes it into the pocket of his shorts, and follows. I move faster, towards the exact spot that I want to fall backwards on to. The farmer will go berserk if he sees us. "Here," I say. "Here's good."

I don't quite fall back like I would on snow, but I let my limbs go loose and do a controlled descent. The wheat is scratchy on the bare skin of my arms and legs as I flatten it. Some of the stems poke me quite hard. I picture myself from above. A wheat angel. A fallen angel.

"This is mad," says Brandon. He's beside me, lying down, moving his arms. He looks different. Happy. He laughs and turns his head to make eye contact through the spiky stalks between us.

"There are probably snakes and mice living in here, aren't there?" I say.

"What?" He leaps up. "Whoa. You didn't have to say that."

I stand up more sedately, squinting at the flattened shapes, to see if there's anything angel-like about them.

They don't look like much at all, and now I feel a bit bad about flattening the wheat. I say, "We'd better go back. There must be a place we can squeeze through on to the road."

Walking out of the wheat is harder work than going the other way. I can hear the hum of insects, and bits of rustling that might be me, or might be animals moving through the stalks. Once I'm free, I brush off the little pieces that are all over me, and pull at the stubborn pieces in my hair. I pick up the map, compass and pen and check out a section of hedge that's thinner than the rest, while Brandon is still de-stalking himself.

"Here," I call. I push the thorny hedgerow as far back as I can and move sideways into the small gap. A couple of thorns grasp my T-shirt. Brandon comes over and helps to release me.

"Thanks." Freed, I shimmy further through the gap. "Watch out!" I shout as I realize I can't hold the hedge any more, and it pings back.

Brandon ducks. "That nearly blinded me. You owe me now."

I step down into the lane. "What do I owe you?" I call.

There's a pause before the answer comes back: "You have to subscribe to my blog. I need more followers."

"What do you blog about?" I ask as I look around. I'm surrounded by hedges and lanky stemmed flowers. One way there's nothing but fields. In the other direction there are roofs and a church spire.

Brandon emerges under thorny branches, part sliding on his back, part limbo dancing, and I grapple with the hedge once more to help him through.

"Trailers. Film trailers, book trailers. Not the sort with wheels."

"Oh." I think about this. "Right. Trailers."

"It's niche."

"I'll check it out."

"Yeah, you have to." He gives a final shake of his hair to rid it of wheat.

We walk along the road, and as it curves round, we see a large red-brick house, and behind a wall we hear the splashing, shrieking sounds of kids in a pool.

"Can you imagine having your own pool?" says Brandon.

"We used to have one," I say. "Until we moved."

"You must have been sad to leave that pool."

"No. I wasn't." I say it too sharply.

I can tell he's working up to say something. It takes him several seconds.

"Did your sister drown? Is that why you're a swim-squad kid who's scared of water?"

I nod. I can't believe he's worked it out.

"Were you there?"

"No," I say.

I hate myself for lying.

ten

Brandon and I climb back over the five-bar gate into Morley Hill grounds.

"Let's say we got lost," Brandon says.

"And that we lost the quiz."

Brandon pushes it further down the pocket of his shorts.

The red-T-shirted instructor is sitting on a deckchair next to the main dining area and is too busy texting to ask what happened to us, why Danielle isn't with us, or to mind that we haven't done the quiz. He's happy to tick us off his list, take back the map, compass and pen, and return to his texting. "Well done, guys!" he says as an afterthought when we walk away in the direction of the yellow dining room for cake.

There's a self-consciousness between us now. We've shared something yet we still hardly know each other. We take a small path off the main one because it cuts off a corner. Much further up the path are two people walking away from us, holding hands.

At the same moment, Brandon and I realize who it is. Joe and Fay.

We look at each other and Brandon raises his eyebrows.

Joe's stride is long and bouncy compared to Fay's small steps, and as they reach the top of the small path to join the main one again, Joe pulls his hand away from Fay's. I slow down, not wanting them to know we were behind them, and Brandon matches my pace.

"D'you think they make a good couple?" I ask.

Brandon pulls his head back slightly. Surprised. "Er . . . yeah. Maybe. I don't know. What do you think?"

"I'm not sure," I say.

"Sometimes you can't properly explain why someone fancies someone else," says Brandon. He sounds as if he knows what he's talking about.

As soon as we step into the dining room, we're greeted with a loud rendition of "Happy Birthday". I step back and let Brandon cringe alone. The cake is home-made, large and chocolate. Pippa lights the candles and tells him to make a wish. I wonder if it's only me who hates wishes. If there are other people who think wishes are thoughts that hurt.

Pippa cuts the cake up into small pieces and Brandon hands it out on napkins. She announces that tonight's entertainment will be karaoke and goes on to introduce a man with a closely shaved head. That's how the workshop on Coping with Difficult Feelings begins, before everyone's been given cake and before anyone has a chance to leave the dining room. Brandon sends me a that's-all-I-need-on-my-birthday face, which makes me smile.

The man tells us he's worked with lots of kids in our position blah blah, everyone is different blah blah, all feelings after bereavement are normal blah blah. Stages of grief. Blah argh. He holds up a book that a client of his made about their dad. Favourite memories. The usual. Write a letter that you don't send. I've heard all this stuff from the counsellor at my old school already. She wanted me to do a journal of feelings. She even gave me a notebook. I thought about doing it, but then I pictured Mum or Dad or anyone else finding it and seeing my ugly feelings laid bare.

When we're all back in our room, I read through Mum's texts, sent throughout the day. Scintillating snippets of news such as *Oscar & I went shopping for new trainers* and *Back from the park.* A smug one from Oscar, sent on Mum's phone: *In Nando's.* In between these are the anxious ones... *Watch out for undercooked food (especially chicken). Make sure you lock your bedroom door at night.*

After I've texted Mum to tell her nothing bad's happened and I'm still alive, my fingers hover over the MessageHound app that Luisa and I used to use instead of texting. We had a private group, just her and me. We liked

MessageHound because of the logo, a cute cartoon dog with a piece of mail in its mouth and a tail that wagged when you had a message. The dog sat with a dejected face when you hadn't messaged for seven days or more. There was also the important fact that you had to log in with a username and four-digit passcode so that Mum, who liked to monitor my mobile phone activity when we first set it up, couldn't see what we were saying about her, Dad and Oscar. Back then, she was under the happy illusion that if she had my phone password, she had access to everything. We texted too, of course, when we couldn't be bothered to tap in our passcode, but MessageHound was our thing. One day soon, I'm going to delete the app, but I can't bring myself to do it yet.

I open it and look through some of the photos – we particularly liked to save the stupid ones there. The last one posted is of Luisa wearing a king-size duvet cover. More precisely, she has a duvet cover over her. The floral pattern of it is faintly visible even though it's inside out. I rested her sunglasses over the top and she has her arms outstretched. A ghost in shades. I posted it straight to MessageHound. About an hour and a half later she was dead.

After two deep breaths, I type.

SKYE: I miss you Luisa.

If that Coping with Difficult Feelings Guy knew I'd done that, he'd say it was because of his talk. Maybe he'd be right, but the truth is I've been gearing up to do it for months. To leave Luisa a final message. MessageHound is the best place I know for feeling that she's near me. The app's passcode-protected, better than a notebook. And I've cheered up the cartoon dog. He's standing up again, looking hopeful.

"Skye, which top d'you think I should wear for the karaoke?" asks Fay. She has an array of them laid out on her bed.

I close the app and roll over. "Are you and Joe in a thing?" I ask.

Fay picks up a white shirt, embroidered with clumsy flowers. The sort of garment that she probably thinks is cute but so isn't. "Why d'you think that?"

"I saw you two holding hands."

Danielle stops whatever she's doing on her phone. "Ooooh, Fay! Tell us more."

That was stupid of me, to mention it in front of Danielle.

Fay's face turns red and she holds the shirt up against her. "It was nothing," she says.

"We need some gossip. This place is so dull," says Danielle.

Fay stiffens. She crumples the top into her lap. "I think he likes me but I'm not sure. Don't say anything, will you? Promise?"

"Calm down," says Danielle. "Don't flatter yourself. It's not that interesting anyway."

"Not that embroidered top," I say. "Show me some other options."

*

For the karaoke, the tables in the yellow dining room have been stacked to one side and the chairs have been arranged in groups. There's a big screen on the wall that currently shines blue and the main lights have been switched off. The place smells of the chicken and rice dish we ate earlier, mixed in with floor cleaner.

Fay chats with Pippa at the front while the room fills up. Danielle sits next to me, and when Joe comes in, he takes the chair on the other side.

"Don't you want to sit next to Fay?" asks Danielle in her less-than-subtle way.

Joe looks surprised. "Are you trying to get rid of me?" He smells of aftershave and clean clothes. He waves over the other two boys from his room, Henry and Rohan, to come and sit with us. When Brandon arrives, there are no more free seats near me. Before I can catch his eye and mime to him that he should pull up a chair, he goes to the front. Fay finishes her conversation with Pippa and is clearly upset to see that not only have I failed to save her a seat, I'm also sitting next to Joe. I pull a face to say I'm sorry.

Pippa and the high-ropes instructor start the karaoke by belting out some horrendous country and western song that I recognize from one of Dad's playlists. Danielle films it on her phone, until Pippa notices and makes a motion with her hand to stop. Everyone applauds loudly – Joe throws in a few whoops – then when Pippa asks who'd like to sing next, there's total silence.

Fay stands up. She finally chose a short floppy beige dress. Unfortunately there's every possibility that she'll blend into the mushroom-coloured walls.

"Brilliant. Thank you, Fay," says Pippa. She ushers her to the microphone, and they whisper song choices for a few minutes, before the screen flashes up a title: "Dream a Little Dream of Me".

Danielle groans. "God. That's typical of Fay."

At first Fay's voice is how I expected it to be – babyish and quiet – but after a few bars, it becomes stronger and more surprising. The notes are spot-on and pure. She nails it. When she finishes to enthusiastic clapping, she reverts to her diminished self, drooping one shoulder and screwing up her face in a mixture of pleasure and embarrassment.

Joe and Henry go up next, and sing so out of time and tune that people laugh. They overact and howl the high notes.

Pippa says she wants everyone to be brave and have a go. She suggests a girls' group followed by a boys' group.

Singing in a group doesn't feel brave, until I'm at the front with the four other girls and I recognize the prickling sensation in my armpits. I concentrate on reading the repetitive lyrics, and can't believe how long it takes for the song to be over. When I sneak a glance at Brandon, he's looking at me. I wish I was doing something other than mumbling tunelessly.

The boys shout their way through a rap, and then Danielle decides she's going to sing on her own. Rohan leans across to ask me if I know anything about the jump from the high tower at the end of the holiday, and he tells me about a sky-dive his sister did. It takes me a few seconds to notice what Danielle's singing.

It's the soundtrack to last summer. The song that Luisa played on repeat in Mum's car. The one that she couldn't stop humming round the house.

I finish the conversation and close my eyes. I can see Luisa singing in the car with the windows open. Her hair is flapping about because she's forgotten a hair elastic, and she doesn't want to close the window.

A wave of missing her crashes over me.

I feel a hand on my back. "Skye?" I open my eyes, and through the tears I see Joe. He offers me a tissue.

His hand returns to my back. It makes a circular movement, then goes up to my shoulder. He gives me a sort of shoulder massage. At first it's comforting, but then it makes me feel awkward. Uncomfortable. I pull away, but his hand goes to my waist on the opposite side, touching me under my T-shirt. I move suddenly, across to Danielle's empty chair, without looking at him. I pretend it's because I can see Danielle singing better from that chair. When Danielle comes back to her seat, I have to return to my own.

Joe doesn't say anything and neither do I.

eleven

It's hard to drift off to sleep. I lie in bed and think about Joe being touchy-weird with me. He could see I was upset and was being kind. Almost certainly. Was it so bad, his probing hand on my skin? Have I become afraid of intimacy or something?

I wish I could talk to Fay about it, and ask how Joe is with her. How he makes her feel. She's fast asleep with her bedraggled toy rabbit on the pillow next to her, but I couldn't see that conversation taking place even if she was awake.

It's only semi-dark in the room because light from the corridor seeps under the door, and outside it's not fully dark. In the bed beside me, Danielle is doing something on her phone.

I pick up my own phone from the chest of drawers beside my bed. I'd like to message Annika, see if she still remembers who I am after I moved school last October and dropped out of her life completely, but I don't know what to say.

My phone vibrates as a text comes through. *Night Skye xxx*. Mum again. She never tires of her weak joke about the night sky.

I force myself to message back three matching kisses. Those three Xs will help her sleep.

"Skye?" says Danielle. She's rolled over to bed to face me. "Want to come outside for a fag with me?"

I'm wide awake, and I need distraction from the tightness in my chest. "All right."

Danielle finds a zip-up hoody to wear over her pyjama top, and I pull on a thin cardigan. We slip our feet into flip-flops in silence, not wanting to wake Fay. Danielle's all set to go, but I find a biro on top of Fay's chest of drawers and an old receipt from my purse. I lean on the countertop and scrawl *GONE FOR WALK. DON'T WORRY, S + D.*

"She's not going to wake up," says Danielle by the door. I pin down the message on Fay's chest of drawers with her phone. A text message flashes up without making a noise. It's from Joe: *Dream of angels Fay x.*

Yuck.

"For God's sake, Skye. Get a wriggle on."

Outside the air is fresh and cool. I let Danielle lead the

way. She takes us to a bench by the mini go-kart track. It's relatively secluded here, on the edge of the wooded area and not overlooked by any windows. She places two cigarettes in her mouth and lights them both. Her face, lit up by the flame, is make-up free, younger looking.

She hands me a cigarette.

"Thanks." I don't really want it, but I want to be here. "It's really peaceful," I say, and I lean back against the bench.

"It's like the cemetery where my mum is," says Danielle. "Sometimes I go there at night. Climb over the fence and sit near her." She takes a deep draw of the cigarette. "You'd think it'd be creepy but it's not."

I nod and gaze at the trees, at the silently moving leaves. Only thirty or forty minutes away from here is Pitford. At night, the distance seems closer.

"But those wind chimes relatives leave on the graves. . ." Danielle says. "What's that all about? They do my head in. After a bit, though, you don't notice them, do you?"

I hold my cigarette and watch the ash forming at the end. Luisa was turned into ashes. Mum and Dad can't decide where to scatter them.

"I sometimes talk to my mum in the cemetery," says Danielle. "Stupid, isn't it?"

I shake my head. "Not any more stupid than writing a letter to her, like that man suggested."

Danielle taps her ash on to the earth. "Mum wrote me letters before she died." She takes a drag and sighs out the smoke. "They're cards, really. She wasn't much of a writer. She wrote ten of them. I was supposed to open them on my birthdays and at Christmas. I found where my dad had hidden them and opened them in one go. Got it out of the way. They all said the same thing: she hopes I'm happy." She rolls her eyes. "Not very imaginative, was it?"

We watch a bird land on the track. It stares at us.

"My sister and I had MessageHound," I say. Danielle doesn't look as if she knows it. "A closed group, just the two of us," I continue. I try breathing smoke out of my nose. "Anyway, I messaged her today. Like a final thing."

"What did you say? *Having a blast at Bereavement Camp. Wish you were here?*"

"Not quite."

We sit in silence for a bit, until Danielle says, "Poor Joe, huh?" She thinks I haven't caught up with her line of thought, so she adds, "Girlfriend committing suicide. That's got to be tough. D'you think he feels guilty? Like he could have talked her out of it?"

"Dunno." I grind the rest of my cigarette under my flip-flop and chuck the remains of it into the nearest bush. "He fancies himself as a smooth talker, so maybe."

Danielle snorts, then says, "What about Brandon? You look pretty tight with him."

Brandon's easy to be with. Friendly. I don't want him examined under Danielle's scorching spotlight, so I nod and say "Yeah" in a vague way.

I pull my cardigan more tightly round me and bring

my legs up on to the bench, huddling into a ball. It's cold. "You ready to go back?" I ask.

"In a moment." She finishes her cigarette and leaves the fag end on the ground. I wait for her to chuck it somewhere more discreet and when she doesn't, I do it myself.

"You worry too much," says Danielle. "Chill." She's fiddling with a small hinged tin. "Want one of these?" She holds up the open tin. It's packed with round white flat chalky tablets, and smaller cylindrical ones with a smooth pale blue coating.

"What are they?"

"Take a blue one."

I look at her, confused.

She laughs. "They help me sleep." She takes a blue pill, pops it into her mouth, and swallows.

In my entire life, I've only ever had medicines meant for children, in liquid form and flavoured strawberry or banana. "OK," I say, because I want to sink my head into my pillow and sleep solidly without nightmares. I crave one normal wake-up-feeling-refreshed night. "Thanks."

It tastes of nothing on my tongue, but I can feel it there, the smoothness dissolving as we walk back to the accommodation block. Danielle is talking about tomorrow and I can't concentrate on what she's saying because I've changed my mind. I don't want to swallow the rest of this drug, whatever it is. It might not even be a sleeping pill. As we walk past the flower bed, I spit it out, watching it fall between stems and out of sight.

"What did you do that for?" says Danielle. "D'you know how much those cost? The hassle of getting them?"

"Sorry," I say, but I'm glad that half the capsule is dissolving in the earth and not me.

Danielle walks on ahead of me, as if I'm not there.

twelve

My thoughts are darting in every direction as I lie on my bed. They skitter and scatter like insects. Joe's hands on my skin. Wind chimes in a cemetery. Luisa in a duvet cover and sunglasses. Metallic pink envelopes. Red water. Mum screaming at me, *"Why didn't you do something?"*

I turn over my pillow, plump it up and slam my forehead into it. The insects slow down. All my limbs are heavy, and a sleepy fog descends.

When I wake, I'm thirsty. I stumble into the bathroom to scoop water from the tap into my mouth and flop back on the bed. I have the sensation of being cut off from reality, my worries floating out of reach. It's not morning but I have no clue if I've slept for five minutes or five hours. I switch on my phone. 4.37 a.m. In the right-hand corner of the screen a cartoon dog is wagging his tail.

I have a MessageHound message. Is this a dream where I feel awake? I'm too muddled to think properly.

My finger moves independently to my brain, tapping in four digits.

LUISA: Hello Skye. I miss you too.

A message from my dead sister. My head is fuzzy but immediately I know this is a strange and wondrous thing to happen. I realize a message from Luisa is what I've been waiting for all these long months.

I type back, my fingers stabbing at the keys.

SKYE: Is it really you?

My eyes are too heavy to keep open, and my thoughts drift.

Fay's twinkly music alarm wakes us. Danielle swears and rolls over, and Fay goes to the bathroom. Soon the only sound in the room is the muffled noise through the wall of water drumming on to the shower tray.

"That . . . pill you gave me. . ." I say in a croaky voice to Danielle's back. "I feel really rough. Like I've had the craziest night."

She doesn't answer.

There's a ping from my phone. I press the home button and there, like a resurfaced memory, is the MessageHound dog wagging his tail. Is my phone having a meltdown, re-receiving messages that were sent ages ago? I touch the icon and tap in my passcode. Words spring up in the heart-jerkingly familiar font.

LUISA: Yes it's me. Don't freak out.

Everything slows. My blood. My breathing. My brain.

I scroll back and the memory returns to me with a jolt: during the night Luisa messaged me and I messaged back. This is a closed, passcode-protected chat. Only two people have ever had access to it. Me and Luisa. There's a big padlock symbol in the corner of each text box.

What does this mean? Has Luisa, my clever, clever sister, found a way to communicate with me? From wherever she is – or the part of her that's still her? I touch the words on the screen, inadvertently causing them to expand into huge letters. I wish each letter were a real, solid thing that I could pick up and hold. She reached me. She somehow made these precious words appear in my phone. I'm almost weightless with elation.

It's hard to believe this has happened. I've heard about signs from the other side, white feathers floating out of nowhere, a sudden change in temperature, flickering lights. But this? A proper message via the internet – I've never heard of this.

Do I believe in life after death? I want to. I really want to.

But I'm not sure what I believe.

The elation transitions into uncertainty. Perhaps this isn't a good thing. Fear clutches me as I sit up. What if it's a bad thing? I don't know what to do. If only I could think more clearly. I breathe in through my nose for a count of five, let my breath out in a rush and type.

SKYE: How do I know it's you?

Fay comes out of the bathroom, locates her hairdryer and turns it on to full power, and Danielle rearranges her pillow so it's over her head. I wait hunched up over the phone, but the screen stays the same until it goes black from inactivity.

thirteen

Yew Tree House, last summer

Luisa's boyfriend, Nico, is driving her home for the summer. They've been going out for a while but we haven't met him yet. She messages me to say they're near Pitford and I wait on the landing for the car to turn into the drive. It's silver, and very flash for a student. Before I hurtle downstairs, I watch Nico step out on to the gravel. He has shiny leather shoes with little tassels on them.

I've seen photos of him on MessageHound so I already know he's fit, with a sharper haircut than anyone round here. As he re-tucks his dark purple shirt into his smart jeans, he looks up at the house and sees me at the window. Stares at me unsmiling. I shrink away and move slowly downstairs, my desire to rush all gone, while Mum shouts, "They're here!"

Luisa looks different. Less studenty, more serious. When I fling my arms round her, I can tell she's lost weight.

"Nico, this is Skye," says Luisa.

"Nice to meet you," he says, looking past me to Mum and Dad. He shakes their hands and says hello to Oscar, who's gone all shy. Nico curves one hand round Luisa's backside and smiles with cold eyes.

Later, after lunch, with Mum doing most of the talking, Nico and Luisa go out in the car, and I feel lonelier than I did before she came home.

The next day, Luisa says, "You mustn't say anything to Mum and Dad, but I'm not going back to uni."

We're floating on two lilos in the pool. It's the first time we've been totally on our own since she's been home. Everyone else is out and Nico has driven on to his parents' house.

I roll off my lilo and swim up to her, pleased she won't be going away again, but worried for her. "Did you fail your exams?" I ask.

"No, but uni's not for me. I want to work. Make money."

Is this about Dad's business? "Why?"

I wait for her to tell me more. When she stays silent, sculling her lilo further away from me, I say, "Why haven't you told Mum and Dad about uni?"

"They've got enough problems right now. I'll tell them soon, after Oscar's operation."

His operation is weeks away.

She doesn't like me coming into her bedroom any more, or me being anywhere near her when she speaks on her phone for hours. When Nico comes round, he calls me "the shadow". Luisa says I'm being oversensitive when I tell her I hate it. They go to parties, and out for the day in his silver car. They speak in a kind of code, which according to Mum shows they're a close couple.

"You're different since going to uni," I tell Luisa as I braid her hair in front of the TV before she goes out to a party. I watch how the different shades of brown and gold reveal themselves as I select and twist the various sections.

"What d'you mean?" she asks, turning her head slightly.

"Not so . . . interested" is the best I can come up with. Before, she would have reacted differently to my story about Annika's sister having her belly button pierced, or the mad things customers say to me when I'm working at the farm shop. "By the way, Toby really wants to see you."

Luisa sighs. "He needs to move on."

"He only wants to say hello." I finish her hair and show her the back by taking a photo of it on my phone.

"Thanks," says Luisa. She slips her feet into fancy flip-flops, new and expensive. Her toenails alternate red and pink, and clash with the orange dress she's wearing.

"I'll find you an orange nail varnish if you like," I say.

"Don't bother," she says. "This is my signature toe look this summer."

I laugh. She always has a nail varnish thing going on. "You should open a nail bar," I say. "I could help you. Our own business."

"Actually, I..." She hesitates, then says, "I'm trialling a nutrition supplement business. Tablets for amazing skin and general health."

Nutrition? Luisa mostly lives off salt and vinegar crisps, and Nutella and banana sandwiches.

"Why didn't you tell me?" I ask.

"Because the supplements haven't received the final-final approval from the government. It's a secret thing."

"Oh," I say. "Well, I don't mind helping."

"No," Luisa says sharply. "I don't need help."

"Don't be horrible. Let me do something."

"I suppose you could help me with deliveries," she says. Doubtfully.

So the next day we go out in Mum's car. Luisa drives fast down the country roads, with the music pumped up high, singing along, air conditioning on and the front windows open. When instructed, I leap out of the front passenger seat and post pink metallic envelopes through letter boxes or to people waiting in prearranged places. It's fun.

fourteen

Now

"Is it OK if I come to breakfast with you?" asks Fay. Her face is contorted with a nervous I-don't-mind-if-you-say-no expression.

"Sure," I say, and her face smooths out again. I wonder if she can see how jittery I am, incapable of concentrating on anything other than my phone. At least I'll avoid looking like a complete loner in the main dining hall again. Or worse, having to hang out with Joe. Of course, now I think about it, the whole reason Fay's making the breakfast trip is probably because she's hoping to hang out with him.

I wouldn't mind sitting next to Brandon, but he's

nowhere to be seen, so when I've selected my breakfast, I find a table for two at the back of the hall and ignore Fay's look of disappointment when she finds me. She sips her orange juice, and picks out all the grapes from her bowl of fruit salad. To begin with, I assume it's because she hates grapes; then, as she eats them in her fingers, one by one, I realize that's the only part of the fruit salad she likes.

My phone is in my pocket, vibrate and volume on maximum. "Have you ever thought your dad was trying to contact you?" I ask. "You know, with a sign or something."

Fay shakes her head. "I'd like him to though."

I cut my pancake with the side of my fork and tuck my other hand in my pocket, round my phone. "You wouldn't be scared?"

"Depends," says Fay. She pulls the corners of her mouth down as she considers the question further. "It depends what he wanted to say to me. Why?"

"I had a dream last night about how my sister was trying to contact me."

And two actual messages on my phone from her.

"You should sign up for a one-to-one counselling session this afternoon," says Fay. She follows the journey of a chunk of pancake and maple syrup as it travels from my plate into my mouth.

I shake my head.

"Are you sure?" says Fay.

"Yep." I shrug. "I'm not anti-counselling. Just need

a break from it." Mum was straight in there with the counselling stuff, emailing the pastoral team at school as soon as term started last September. Pretty much once a week until we moved I sat on a swivel chair in a tiny office in the head's corridor mumbling to a woman with a cycle-helmet haircut. I tried to explore my feelings, come up with strategies and set new goals. There was no way I was having counselling at my new school, so now I go fortnightly to a counsellor who sees people at her house. I sit in an armchair and look out at her messy garden, or stare at her desk. At the scruffy folders, gel pens without lids, the Post-it Notes in green, yellow and orange scattered like autumn leaves.

Fay sighs. "I like having someone to listen to me."

I dip a piece of pancake into the pool of syrup.

"I like that counsellors are trained not to be shocked." She squeezes a grape between her thumb and forefinger. "Because I have a secret."

The guilt in her eyes is like a reflection from my own. It startles me.

"I'm responsible for my dad's death. I was arguing with him when he crashed the car," says Fay. "He was distracted. There was a van coming the other way and my dad let the car drift on to the other side of the road…" She squeezes her eyes closed for a second, haunted by a sequence of memories she can never erase. "Counsellors tell me that it's not my fault, but they have to say that. It's their job. I know it's my fault. I was there and they weren't."

She'll have had the "Bad things happen" and "Somehow you have to get past this" talks already, so I say, "That's hard. Is it why you don't eat?"

Fay pushes the pile of grapes away with her crumpled napkin. "When I think about my dad I can't eat." She rearranges the napkin so that it completely covers the grapes. "I was funny about food before, but it's got worse."

I wonder if she judges me like I've judged her, for not being able to stop the unhappiness leaking out in different ways. After I've swallowed my mouthful of flabby pancake, I say, "Since my sister died, food tastes different. Sometimes it doesn't taste of anything at all, but I still eat it."

Fay rubs the corner of her tray where it's chipped. "Sometimes I feel hopeless."

"You're not hopeless," I say. "You're going to be a doctor. You'll make a good doctor."

I try not to say compliments I don't mean. It's mostly impossible, given twenty-first-century social conventions, but I try. Fay will make a good doctor. She cares about stuff, and she's weird enough that people wouldn't feel too weird about themselves in front of her.

"You think so?" Fay smiles, and her face changes shape. Less skull-like.

"Yes, definitely. I used to spend a lot of time around doctors." I know what her next question's going to be, so I pre-empt it. "My brother, Oscar, was born with heart problems."

Out of my side vision, I see a tray and muscly arms. The arms belong to Joe. He's wearing a black T-shirt that says *Dream Big* on it in white letters. I can smell the cleanness of it, the washing detergent. What's he *doing*? We're at a table for two.

"That's sad about your brother," he says. "How old was he when he died?"

"What?"

"Your brother," says Joe, pulling up a spare chair from the next table with one hand while balancing his tray on his other arm. "How old was he?"

"Oscar's nine," I say. "He's still alive."

Joe grimaces as he sits down and manoeuvres his tray on to the table. Unfortunately there is just about room for it. "Oh, sorry." His expression morphs into one of concern. "So how is he? Does he have a decent quality of life?"

"He's fine. Absolutely fine." If Mum were here, she'd be filling him in on the many little details of Oscar's condition, the checks still ahead of him, the necessary precautions, the possibilities of further surgery. But basics: Oscar is fine.

"Wow," says Joe. "Modern medicine is incredible. Morning to you both, by the way." He sits round properly on his chair and pours milk from a little white jug into his bowl of muesli.

Fay watches him in a way that could probably be called staring. She catches me looking at her, and blushes.

"So, is it a genetic thing?" asks Joe. "A family problem?"

Luisa and I had tests and scans, but none of that's any of Joe's business.

"Nah," I say, waving my hand as if the whole thing bores me. "So, who's pumped for the obstacle course this morning?" I glance down at my phone, at the black inactive screen, and for a moment I'm light-headed at the thought of the two messages lurking inside. I think of them waiting there for me, automatically saved, to shock me all over again.

When I mentally join the obstacle-course chat again, Fay is worrying about the chance of rain and whether she'll be made to crawl through mud.

"Today's going to be difficult for me, whether there's mud or not," says Joe through a mouthful of muesli.

"Why?" asks Fay.

I'd have left that sentence hanging myself.

"Today would have been my girlfriend's birthday." Joe loads up another spoon with muesli while Fay communicates panic to me, wanting me to say something first.

I mutter that I'm sorry.

Joe picks his phone up off his tray and shows us his wallpaper photo. It's a head and shoulders shot of a girl in a plain white T-shirt, shiny blonde hair to her shoulders. She's wearing a necklace made from what looks like a shoelace and a triangular wooden pendant with a squiggle on it. Her expression is serious, almost blank. Not your usual surfer-girl attitude. "That's Kyra the day before she died. She would have been sixteen today. I should be celebrating with her."

"She looks nice," says Fay.

I feel sorry for Fay, seeing the dead girlfriend of the boy she fancies.

Joe nods, and carries on holding his phone for us to see.

"Nice necklace," says Fay. She's run out of things to say.

"Thanks," says Joe. "I made it for her." He brings the phone back towards him and fiddles around with it. "I make things for the tourists. Look." The screen is full of beaded and wooden necklaces and carved wooden fish. He swipes the screen again and there's another photo. Him and Kyra in wetsuits with wet hair and surfboards. She's smiling this time. They both are.

"That's my favourite photo," he says. "Look how happy we were."

He makes a choking noise and puts his hand to his eyes so that his thumb is pressing down on one eyelid and a couple of fingers are on the other. "Sorry," he says. "I didn't mean to make a scene." He clamps both hands over his eyes and leans forward with his elbows on the table.

"You're not making a scene," says Fay. "It's OK to cry. I'll get you a napkin. Hang on. I won't be a moment." She hurries off towards the cutlery counter.

If Joe were anyone else, I might put my arm round his shoulder, but the memory of him doing it to me stops me. He's sniffing quietly and I'm still in exactly the same position when Fay rushes back.

"Here you go, Joe," she says.

He raises his head and takes the napkin. Around his eyes his skin is reddish, but I'm struck by the fact that his eyes aren't watery and he doesn't have to blow his nose. If he's trying to make himself look upset, what would the point of that be? An embarrassingly inappropriate form of flirting? I wouldn't put it past him.

"Thanks," he mumbles, and he presses the napkin against his eyes.

Fay looks at me.

"We should get a move on," I say. "Aren't we supposed to be meeting at nine-thirty?"

"You two go on," says Joe. "I'll follow you in a minute."

"If you're sure," says Fay in a very unsure way. "I know this is going to be a very sad day for you, so if there's anything you want me to do. . ."

Joe removes the napkin. His eyes flash with an alarming intensity and his jaw is tight. "Kyra shouldn't have done it. She shouldn't. I don't know why she did it. She had me." He opens up the napkin and buries his face, and this time his sobs sound genuine and heartfelt.

"Don't," says Fay. "Please don't upset yourself."

"I'd like. . ." he says in a wobbly, muffled voice, "a few minutes to myself now."

I motion to Fay that we should leave.

fifteen

"He seemed really angry with Kyra," I say to Fay as we walk back to our room.

"I've heard that people left behind after a suicide are often angry," Fay says. She adds something else but I don't hear because I feel my phone vibrate, and a split second afterwards hear the high-pitched ping that I chose as an audible alert for a MessageHound message.

I slow down. "You go on," I say to Fay. "I've got to check my phone a moment." I wait until she's enough paces away not to be able to see my screen and in almost one touch I tap the dog and input the code.

LUISA: I could tell you your favourite Harry Potter character is Ron Weasley and that my

favourite snack is salt and vinegar crisps, or you could have faith and believe that it's me.

My favourite *Harry Potter* character *is* Ron Weasley, and Luisa *was* addicted to salt and vinegar crisps.

I want so badly to believe it's Luisa writing, that she's hoaxed her own death, Sherlock Holmes–style, and very soon I'm going to work out how she did it. Seeing her familiar profile photo pop up each time makes it easy to imagine it's her sending the messages. In mine I'm wearing a hat with furry antlers and doing an impression of an overexcited buck-toothed reindeer. Luisa is modelling a horrendous bobble hat in hers, knitted by our great-auntie when she heard Luisa was going on the school skiing trip.

I rescued that bobble hat from one of the charity-shop boxes. Luisa had only worn it once for that photo, so it didn't smell of her, and the bobble at the top was coming apart, but I still wanted it.

They were taken the day we set up our MessageHound account. Neither of us ever changed our profile photos; I'm not sure why. We still found them amusing, I guess.

I look down again, and another message pops up.

LUISA: How's life?

Breathe. Breathe. I close the app before dizziness blurs my vision. This is too weird to cope with.

"Don't be late for the obstacle course! No phones allowed. Plenty of time for texting later." Pippa strides past me with her clipboard. "See you there."

*

I don't want anyone to know about the messages, which means I have to act normally. Leaving my phone in the room will help; it'll stop me checking it obsessively.

Danielle has already left when I arrive at the room, and Fay is waiting for me. I bury my phone under a half-dirty T-shirt at the bottom of my suitcase and pull the zip round firmly.

"Teeth, then I'm done," I say to Fay.

In the bathroom, I lean against the sink with my toothbrush and blink away stupid, stupid tears.

The obstacle course begins with a series of car tyres that leads to a ramp with hand- and footholds and a vertical climbing wall the other side. After a short run, there's a plastic tunnel, low hurdles, rope netting over a wooden structure, a set of monkey bars, a steeper ramp with a rope to pull up on and a ladder the other side, and six cones to zigzag round. On a raised platform at the end is a red buzzer the size of a football. There are two identical sets of equipment, side by side.

"This is going to be a team thing, isn't it?" wails Fay as we look at it.

Leaving my phone in the room hasn't made me think about the messages any less.

"Why does everything have to be a competition?" Fay says.

"It's about getting people to want it more, to encourage each other, isn't it? You know, the usual team-building bollocks." I walk with her to the start of the course and stand on one of the car tyres. "Don't worry, it doesn't look too hard. You'll be fine." I resist telling her I'm looking forward to it. I have the same compressed energy inside me that I used to have before a swimming race. Yesterday I had more stamina than Brandon when we ran through the fields. I managed to vault over that five-bar gate with no problem. I'm fitter than I thought.

Thinking about Brandon appears to conjure him up. He walks towards us. In a grey shirt with a stiff white collar, and another tatty pair of shorts.

"Morning!" he says. He seems a lot happier than yesterday. "I'm still trying to get wheat out of my hair. How about you?"

"What are you talking about?" asks Fay.

"Wheat angels," I say. I feel myself reddening. "An orienteering thing."

"There's Joe," says Fay. "I'm going to see if he's OK."

"What's wrong with Joe?" asks Brandon.

I open my mouth to explain but an instructor bellows at us to gather round, and we have to watch a demonstration of the course, and hear how expensive it is to replace the electronic buzzers so there's to be no mucking around with them.

Pippa uses a randomized selection app on her phone to split us into two teams of six. The app allocates me to the same team as Fay and Joe, and the opposite one to Brandon. At least I'm not with Danielle, who's mostly ignoring me this morning. I guess it's because I spat out half her tablet and complained about the effects of the other half.

Nobody appoints Joe as team leader but he assumes the position, telling us we need to go in speed order, the quickest first. Naturally he selects himself to go first. I get the second-to-last slot, behind Kerry, who's wearing flip-flops. Perhaps it's because he's seen me trip over by the pool and fall out of a kayak on a calm lake.

Fay is last. "Do I have to be last?" she asks Joe.

"Trust me, Fay," he says. "I know what I'm doing."

"Everybody ready?" asks Pippa. "Line up in order. Two minutes until I blow my whistle to start."

"Remember, do your best, support your teammates and enjoy yourselves," says the instructor. "And don't lean too heavily on the buzzers."

The whistle goes, and Joe jumps from tyre to tyre, far faster than Nate on the other team. He leaps on to the wooden ramp with ease, scales it, jumps from the top and disappears. Everyone carries on cheering even though we can't see him any more.

"Next people get ready," shouts Pippa. "You have less than one minute before the whistle."

"I hate going last," says Fay.

"Swap with me," I say. "Doesn't matter to me."

Fay frowns. "What will Joe say?"

"Who said he's in charge? If you want to swap, do it."

"If you're sure ... and you don't think Joe will be cross?"

I take hold of her bony arms at the top and propel her past me so that I'm now behind her. "There. Happier?"

She nods. "Thanks."

I turn my attention back to the course in time to see Brandon climbing up the ramp for the other team. There's a mesmerizing quality to the steady way he moves. He's comfortable in his body. Out of everyone in this place, Brandon's probably the one person I'd tell about the messages. If I was telling anyone. Which I'm not, because then I'd have to explain more about what happened last summer.

Soon Fay and I are the only ones on our team left to go. When the whistle blows, Fay shoots off, but although her body is light, it's stiff and awkward and she can't find a rhythm for leaping from tyre to tyre. On the other team, Danielle moves casually. Anyone would think she was checking out a good place to have a fag, but she glides ahead of Fay, who makes several attempts to pull herself up on to the first footholds of the ramp.

"Woooo, Fay!" I scream when she finally has both feet off the ground. As she swivels herself over the top of the ramp on to the climbing wall, I give her a goofy thumbs up.

The last person on the other team is Henry, who's doing warm-up exercises. Trying to put me off.

"Last pair get ready!" shouts Pippa.

I'm ready.

The whistle goes, and I run to the tyres, leaping

between them with enough spring to propel me forward each time. I take the ramp at speed and my hands find their holds first, swiftly followed by my feet. At the top, I clamber down the wall for a bit, then jump, bending my knees on impact. The tunnel smells unpleasant, like the inside of a plastic lunch box. I can feel the hard, knobbly ground as I crawl through it. As I stand up to begin the hurdles, I see Fay through the rope netting. She's standing on the metal step of the monkey bars, one arm holding the side of the frame, the other one reaching towards the first rung of the bars. Joe is talking to her from the sidelines. He's not supposed to be there. He should be with the others at the end of the course. I can't hear what he's saying to her because other people are making noise, but I hear him shout to me, "Why the hell did you swap places?"

"Why are you standing there, putting us off?" I shout back, and leap across the hurdles. Scaling the netting is harder. The monkey bars are now in front of me, and so is Fay, still unable to bring herself to swing across the four bars. The shouting and cheering from everyone who's already completed the course intensifies.

Joe steps forward, over the line he's not supposed to cross. "You two should have listened to me," he says. His voice is quietly furious. "I knew what I was doing."

"It's OK," I say. "I don't mind being last."

"I can't do it," says Fay.

"Listen to me," says Joe. "Trust me. Focus on what I'm

saying: grab that rung with one hand and you'll be able to reach it with the other one."

"I can't."

"Look at me." Joe's voice is softer now. "Look me in the eye."

Fay turns her head. Fixes her eyes on him.

"Do it for me," he says.

With a grunting noise, Fay stretches and leans forward at the same time. She plummets to the ground.

Joe shakes his head. "You didn't trust me enough, did you?"

Henry is doing the hurdles on the other course. He moves on to the monkey bars, barely glancing sideways at us. He reaches for the rope attached to the ramp, and as he gets to the top the waiting crowd go wild. Seconds later, there's a prolonged buzzing sound amid the whoops and cheers.

"Oh, Fay!" Pippa runs up. "Did you fall? Poor you."

I bet she didn't notice that Joe was there before Fay fell. In fact she flashes him a grateful smile for being Mr Kind and Caring.

Fay is on her feet now. "I'm fine. I'll keep going." She walks to the ramp and heaves herself up it. There are more cheers for her, and I get the sympathy clap for coming in last. As Fay presses the buzzer, I yell, "Go us!" I hope next time Joe tries to bludgeon her self-confidence she tells him to piss off.

Joe is there now, and he gives a wolf whistle as I leap on

to the platform and hammer down on the buzzer. "Good effort, team," he says. He turns to hug Kerry, rocking her from side to side.

As I jump down from the platform for Pippa's obligatory group photo, I land badly, twisting my ankle slightly.

"Whoa," says Brandon, there beside me. He puts an arm round my shoulder to support me. The touch of his arm against me is worth the fizzing sting of my ankle. It's different to Joe's touch last night in about a million different ways. I think this means that Joe's a creep and I like Brandon a whole lot more.

The instructor says the course is now open for people to either do at a slower pace or to time themselves.

What I'd like more than anything is to go back to the room and check my phone, but the session isn't over yet. "I'm going to have to sit out for a bit," I say, inspecting my ankle.

"Let's sit on that bench over there," says Brandon.

I wish I knew whether he suggested it because he can't be bothered to do the course again or because he wants to hang out with me. We watch Fay cheer on Joe as he attempts to break the course record for the quickest completion.

A creeping anxiety works its way through my body so that every part of me is on edge. I watch people high-five and slap Joe on the back and I listen to Brandon drum a rhythm on his thigh with his hands, but as soon as Pippa says we're free to go, I'm on my feet and making my way back to the room to see if there are any more messages.

sixteen

Blank. The only new thing showing on my screen is a text from Mum, which I don't even bother to read after skimming the first four words: *I hope you're having. . .*

I open up MessageHound and reread the four messages I've received even though I can remember word for word what they say. Perhaps there won't be any more until I reply to the last one. *How's life?*

I scoot up against the wall at the end of the bed, aware I haven't got long before Fay and Danielle come back and I have to engage with them about the obstacle course or who's doing what activities this afternoon. I open a text box and start typing as fast as my fingers can find the letters.

SKYE: I couldn't sleep for a long time after you died. I gave up swimming because I couldn't get into a pool without having a panic attack. I still have nightmares. We moved and we live in a flat on the edge of London. Dad's business went under and he's looking for work. I changed school mid-year to a different exam syllabus. Everyone thinks I'm a major geek and social reject because I don't talk much and I keep my head down.

My eyes flicker over the chunk of text, and immediately I see how foolish and exposing my words are. Of course I've always known deep down that these messages can't be coming from Luisa. There are unexplained things in life, but messages via the internet are generated by people or computers, and I'm pretty certain that a computer isn't composing these messages. I admit it: I wanted to believe in a miracle.

A real-life person is writing messages to me, pretending to be my dead sister. Clumsy on the keyboard now, I scramble for the backspace key and hold it down, watching as it vacuums up my sentences until the text box is empty again. I have the same reeling sensation that I had when Oscar once kicked a football at my head. The same slowness to realize what's going on, but this time accompanied by thudding fear. Someone has hacked into Luisa's account and is deliberately messing with my brain.

What do they want? Twisted fun – or something more sinister?

How's life? What does that *mean*?

There hasn't been a day when I haven't thought of the sickening thud and the pool of red water, and heard Mum's screaming in my head. Remembered the smell of chlorine as I bunched myself up as tightly as I could. The dull pain in my forehead as I pressed it down on to my kneecap.

SKYE: Go away.

I send it before I'm tempted to type something far blunter, which might provoke the creep at the other end.

Danielle comes bursting through the door, and I close the app. "You missed two Blues having a fight by the volleyball pitch. Pippa was blowing her whistle at them. Hilarious." She sees that I don't find it as amusing as she does. "What's the matter? Still tired from those dreams you couldn't handle?"

Fay comes in. "That obstacle course was horrible." She sits on the end of my bed and goes into a long explanation of why she hasn't got the strength in her arms to do the monkey bars. I let her talk while my finger hovers over the *Delete App?* button. If I press, will there be a ghostly echo somewhere of all the messages Luisa and I ever sent to each other? I wonder if they'd be recoverable from my phone's internal memory. Like when the police raid houses for dodgy computers and teams of experts can see exactly what someone's been up to, even though that person got a tip-off and deleted all the files before the police rammed the door down.

I can't do it. I can't bear to lose the messages from my once-real sister.

Danielle changes in front of us, out of her T-shirt and leggings into shorts and a sleeveless top. "I'm going for lunch. See you," she says, and bangs the door shut behind her.

Fay's monologue grinds to a halt and she goes into the bathroom. As I chuck my phone down beside me, it pings.

LUISA: You have it easy compared to me.

I flinch from the accusing words. Easy? I'm not dead, that's true, but I have to live with what happened every single day, and witness the effects of it on others. If I could relive that day last summer, I would. I'd relive it over and over until I could make things right. But there are no second chances. This is how it will always be.

However upsetting these messages are, I can't delete them. They're evidence. I have to find out who this person pretending to be Luisa is.

Fay comes out of the bathroom. "If we don't go for lunch now we'll be late."

The afternoon activities are lawn games and a fifty-minute slot with one of two specialist grief counsellors. Lawn games according to Fay are croquet, badminton and use of the giant outdoor chess set. According to Danielle they're a euphemism for sunbathing, though that's unlikely to happen given the grey clouds visible from the yellow dining room. Pippa says the counselling is optional but she floats around during dessert with her clipboard trying to entice everyone to sign up. I can't imagine why anyone would want to specialize in grief.

My phone is still and silent in the pocket of my shorts. I want to send a message without being watched, so I tell Fay I need to return to our room, muttering that I need to sort out my trainers before the afternoon session.

Brandon's further down the table. As I rush past him, I catch his eye and he mouths, *You OK?* Is it my imagination or does he spend quite a chunk of his time watching me?

I nod, and run through the drizzle back to the accommodation block. As soon as I'm in the room, I reach for my phone. No new messages. I'd have heard the alert if there'd been one. I hardly said a word at lunch I was concentrating so hard on listening out for it.

After crash-diving on to the bed, I type my message:

SKYE: Tell me who you really are and what you want.

I press send with a firm, decisive tap, then reach for my earphones and listen to my playlist on shuffle, each ping of the music making me think I have a reply.

"Skye!" Fay's voice cuts through the music.

I take out an earphone.

"What are you doing? You've been gone ages," she says. I see she's holding a partially closed umbrella that's dripping water on to the floor. "Pippa asked me to fetch you. We had to abandon the lawn games because of the rain. We're in the common room instead."

"How exciting," I say.

"Playing board games."

I face-plant into my pillow.

In the end I only agree to go to the common room because Fay is practically hysterical at the thought of telling Pippa that she failed in her task of retrieving me. We bunch together under the umbrella and scuttle along the rain-darkened paths.

The common room smells of damp socks and old cardboard. It looks like the old people's social clubs you see on television, with lots of bleak-looking tables and stackable chairs. There's a massive cork noticeboard, covered sparsely with curling, faded photos, a floral thank-you card and a pizza takeaway menu. The other wall decorations are a flat-screen TV and laminated rules. *Please pack away all board games after use! No takeaways to be consumed on the premises! If you need change for the vending machine, please ask the reception staff (nicely!).*

I look around but there isn't a vending machine. There's a large built-in cupboard with open doors, rammed with games. An instructor is sorting through it. Most of the Yellows, including Brandon and Joe, are crowded round a table playing or watching a card game. Judging by the arguing and squeals, it's a tense one. Danielle is videoing it, winding Henry up because she's filming everyone's cards from behind. On a separate table, Kerry and Alice are inserting plastic discs at random into a Connect Four frame.

"Thanks, Fay!" Pippa comes at us with her clipboard. She takes the umbrella from Fay, who drifts off towards the cupboard.

"Skye, you're not on my list for the counselling," says Pippa. "Would you like me to try and squeeze you in?"

"No, thanks," I say.

Pippa nods and tells me I need to find myself a team for the quiz night later on. "It's a joint activity – I'm hoping for a yellow team in the top three! Right, I'm off to report a leaking shower to the maintenance department."

Fay waves a chess set at me. "We can do the mini version until the weather clears up!"

I shake my head.

"Scrabble? *Please?*"

I console myself that Fay has her counselling appointment in twenty minutes, but the time drags as she ponders each move, and my thoughts return to the last two messages I sent. Have they been read yet? What could I have written that would have made me sound more in control?

As soon as Fay leaves, I tip the Scrabble letters into a pile, and make a sentence on the board: YOU DO NOT SCARE ME. I take a photo on my phone, bringing it down quickly into my lap when I see Joe in my peripheral vision. With a manic circular movement, I break up the sentence and begin to scoop up the letters to pack them away.

"Scrabble for one?" says Joe. "Come and join the card game."

"Hey, Joe!" calls Henry from the card table. "Let's go bomb into the pool in the rain."

The instructor at the cupboard looks round. "Er, guys, you'd need a lifeguard and a—"

Henry stands up. "Who's in?"

"Everyone except Skye," calls Danielle. "She won't go in the pool when it's sunny so you won't get her in now."

I fold the Scrabble board in half and pull the box towards me.

"Give her a break," calls Brandon. Loudly. "Her sister drowned in a pool last summer, OK?"

The air in front of me wobbles, but I keep packing everything away.

Joe's still next to me. "I don't think she wants her story broadcast, mate," he says.

My head drops so no one can see my burning face. Confiding in Joe about Luisa less than twelve hours after arriving here and then telling Brandon too were the dumbest moves of the holiday. There's stillness in the room, followed by murmuring. A headache develops above my right eye as I fiddle around with the Scrabble letters.

The instructor asks for everyone to listen to him a moment, and announces that since the rain's stopped, croquet is back on, and would we all like to go outside, taking care not to slip on the wet grass. There's lots of moaning until Rohan says something about croquet wars which makes people head noisily outside.

I stay and pack up the Scrabble. Very slowly. When I've placed the lid on the box, I turn the whole thing over and read the game description on the back.

"Skye?"

I flicker my eyes up and see Brandon, and look back down again. Talk about awkward.

"I'm sorry. I didn't mean to blurt that out."

We're the only ones here now, and his voice seems extra-loud in the silence. I give a brief nod to indicate *Apology accepted*. I'm not going as far as saying, "Don't worry about it."

"Can I sit down?"

"I'm a bit busy."

"I want to ask you something. It won't take long."

"Go on, then," I say, and finally look at him as he sits. I wait for the question, ready to shoot it down.

"You said you used to live near here. . ."

Stop talking about this.

"There's not much going on this afternoon," continues Brandon. "If it's not too far, I wondered if you wanted to go and see your old house?"

"What? Why would I want to do that?"

"It helped me to see mine. I know it's not the same. Nobody drowned. But my brother died there. When my parents split up, we moved and I dreamed about the house all the time. I went back once and I saw it was just bricks and stuff and it shifted a few things for me in my head."

I've thought about seeing Yew Tree House again. I

discussed it with my new counsellor, thought about what it would be like to go back, either now, one year on, or in the future. There were two ways I imagined it – either going with Mum or Dad, who'd be crying uncontrollably, or with Oscar when he was older and I was trying to explain what I'd done. Or not done.

What would it be like to go with Brandon? "There's a big fence," I say. "I wouldn't be able to see the swimming pool. Only the top of the changing room and the house."

Brandon nods towards my phone. "We could find out about train and bus times."

Why are you pushing me to do this?

"I heard we're only allowed out of the grounds between three and five to visit the village shop."

"We wouldn't sign out. We wouldn't go through the reception building – we'd go over that gate we found. No one would miss us."

What if I bumped into someone I knew? Everyone knows we moved away – wouldn't they think it was strange that I'd come back to look at my old house? But if it made a difference to my nightmares it might be worth it. It's so close, Yew Tree House, close enough to feel it luring me back. But what if seeing the house freaked me out and added a whole new horrible layer to my dreams?

"So?" prompts Brandon. "Up to you. What d'you reckon?"

"Not today," I say finally. "I can't face it."

"No worries. It was only an idea," says Brandon. "You

shouldn't force yourself to go unless you really want to." He stands up. "I'll go check out the croquet. See you later."

I nod, and when he's gone, I pick up my phone and move to the tatty sofa at the far end of the room. Curled up so that hopefully nobody will notice me if they glance through the door, I swipe through my photo gallery. There are still photos on my phone that I took before term finished last summer. Selfies of me with Annika. The biology field trip to the coast. Eating Krispy Kreme doughnuts on the field for someone's birthday. Me with Max Tomkins at the swimming club picnic. I enlarge that one. See how over-the-top happy I am that he's kissing me on the cheek for the selfie, and delete it. The swimming crowd did their best after Luisa died, but I slipped away from them, first by not going to so many training sessions, then by having panic attacks in the pool, or by not being able to force myself into the water in the first place. When I moved away they must have been relieved.

I go into MessageHound. No messages. Half of me wishes there would be one so I can have that brief painful hope before my brain reminds me it's all false. I post the You Do Not Scare Me Scrabble sentence, quickly before I can overthink it, then reopen the photo afterwards, imagining the person at the other end receiving it. I hope they're taken aback. Surprised.

Setting the view to slideshow, I watch the MessageHound photos spool through in a loop. Something's bothering me but I can't pinpoint it. Something to do with the photos. I need to back them up, but that's not it. It's about viewing them, and then it occurs to me that the person who hacked into the MessageHound account has access to all the photos and messages linked to it, which means if they'd scrolled back far enough they'd have read Luisa's message about not being able to find salt and vinegar crisps when she was Interrailing, and they'd have seen the photo I sent to her at uni of me dressed up as Ron Weasley for Annika's *Harry Potter* party.

And that means anyone could be the imposter.

seventeen

Yew Tree House, last summer

Luisa storms into my bedroom. I'm lying on the carpet, catching up on series four of an Australian reality show that Max got the whole swim squad into. Luisa is hopping mad. Literally. She can't stand still she's so wound up. In her hand is the pink envelope that I used to place Annika's birthday present in, that I left in the kitchen to give to Annika this evening. Uh-oh.

"Why did you use this envelope?"

I can see it wasn't such a bright idea now. Luisa uses them for her business and they probably cost a fair bit, being that metallic paper. I told her she should have her business name printed on them, and she said she didn't have a business name yet, and no, it wouldn't be a good idea. I guess it's all about the profit.

"I thought Annika would like it," I say. "I've only used one. I'll pay you for it if it's that much of a problem." I press pause on my laptop screen. "I bought her some of those liquorice allsorts earrings in Hoathley," I say, in an attempt to deflect the conversation.

"My business has to be secret," says Luisa.

"Just because your pills aren't approved yet doesn't mean you have to get all paranoid about the envelopes," I say.

"Just accept what I tell you. There are things about my business that you don't need to know." She's speaking slowly and tightly, as if she'd rather be yelling. "You can't leave those envelopes lying around." She shakes her head. "God. If Nico had come round and seen it on the counter, he'd have gone ballistic."

"Nico?" I sit up. "Is he part of the business too?" I'm disappointed because that means he's probably going to be her boyfriend for a lot longer than I was hoping.

Luisa chews her lip. I hold my hand out to take the envelope from her. She rips it open, removes the small tissue-paper-wrapped package, hands me that, and keeps the envelope. Her face is flushed but she's calmer now. Talk about an overreaction. She used to be far more laid back. "No more taking envelopes, Skye. OK?"

She leans against the door frame on the way out. "The nutrition thing is only a sideline. I'm actually thinking of starting a clothes stall in the vintage market."

Sometimes I get the impression that she tests out her half-formed ideas on me, but because she never gives me all the facts, I can never give her the right feedback. "Cool," I say.

Later that morning, I walk up the track to start my shift at the farm shop. It's the first summer I've been paid for helping, which means I'm not allowed to spend my time eating the testers or playing around with the pricing gun. I have to dust and clean, count things in the stockroom, and stack shelves. Occasionally I'm allowed to use the till. I sometimes work with Pat, Toby's mum, or Wendy or Carol from the village, but mostly I'm with Toby.

"Want to come on a delivery when Wendy gets here?" he asks me this morning as I stand on the stool to check the sell-by dates on the chutneys, and arrange them so that customers take the oldest jars first.

That word *delivery* gives me a jolt because I was thinking about Luisa and the pink envelopes.

"Sure," I say.

There are days when I feel more at home here than I do in my own house. There's less tension and I like the orderly chaos. The changing crates of seasonal fruit and veg, and the shelves of preserves, honey, vinegars, olive oils and Lower Road Farm sauces. The displays of locally made cakes and fudge, and the boxes of muddy eggs. I even like the sharp smells which make Oscar wrinkle up his nose every time he comes in – strong cheeses, fresh meat, onions and olives.

When Wendy arrives, I help load up the rusting Volvo

estate car with boxes of produce, dashing from the shop to the car in the drizzling rain. It's good fitness training. I persuade Toby to take Kip, the youngest springer spaniel, with us. He sits in the footwell and rests his chin on my thigh. I play with the little tuft of fur on top of his head, spiking it up, then braiding it.

"Is Lu out with Nasty Nico tonight?" asks Toby as he rattles down the track.

"Don't think so," I say. Nico was here a few days ago, staying for three nights. I hope it's a while before he's back.

"Tell her some of the old gang are meeting at the pub and she should come along," says Toby.

I'm fed up with Toby inviting her to things via me. "Ask her yourself on the way back," I say. "She's at home."

Toby frowns. "You think so?"

We park on our drive an hour or so later, and because Mum's out with Oscar, we bring Kip into the house. Luisa's lying on the sofa in the living room, texting. She looks up as Kip rushes over, paws clicking on the wooden floor.

"Wha—?" says Luisa when she sees Kip, but by then Kip has jumped up on to the sofa and is panting over Luisa's face. "Eughhh. Toby, get him off me. He *stinks*." But Luisa's laughing, and Toby goes over and launches himself on the sofa, kind of on top of her but not, pretending to pull Kip off her. "Eughhh, you stink too, Toby. Have you been delivering cheeses?"

"Come to the pub with me tonight," says Toby. "Naz and the old crew are going to be there."

Luisa sits up and pushes Kip away although Kip thinks it's a game and lunges for the cushion. "I can't," she says. "Nico wouldn't like it."

I don't know if she's lying to avoid going out with Toby, or if she's become the sort of person who puts up with a jealous boyfriend.

"Really?" says Toby, seeming to echo my thoughts.

The rumble of car tyres on gravel make us look at one another as if we're little kids again. Mum's going to hit the roof if she sees Kip in here and chewing on one of her cushions.

"Outside," says Luisa.

We shoot into the garden and arrange ourselves on the patio chairs as if we've been there for a while, even though it's not really a sitting-in-the-garden temperature.

"Hi!" calls Mum. She hears our shouts and comes outside, Oscar trailing after her.

She's pleased to see Toby; less pleased to see Kip digging in a flower bed. Oscar is delighted to see both of them.

"You Mulligans must come for a barbecue at the weekend," Mum says. "We haven't seen you in ages." She talks for a few minutes about the farm with Toby, then goes inside.

"Have you taught Kip any tricks yet?" asks Oscar as Toby heads towards the side gate so he doesn't have to take Kip through the house.

Toby does his best where-have-you-been-all-these-weeks voice. "You mean you haven't seen Kip's incredible weaving talents?" he asks.

Oscar, small and pale, wearing his faded old Spider-Man T-shirt which has been too tight for a long time, jiggles with pleasure.

Toby requests that the three of us stand in a line, side by side, facing the pool, with our legs apart. Then he whistles for Kip, who darts in and out of our legs, with Toby doing a lot of whistling, waving and overpraising.

"Can he jump?" asks Oscar when Kip makes it to the end and sits, hoping for a treat to appear. The Mulligans' other two dogs love to jump.

"Of course," says Toby, and he has Oscar lying on the grass and Kip leaping over him. And then Oscar wants Luisa, Toby and me to lie down next to one another to see if Kip can clear three of us. And because it's Oscar we do. We lie together, but Luisa makes sure that I'm in the middle so that she doesn't have to get too cosy with Toby.

I'm squished between Luisa and Toby, the three of us giggling and squealing because the truth is Kip's a haphazard jumper, liable to land clumsily on top of us. Luisa grabs my hand and gives me the Colton family hand-squeeze – three times in a row as fast as you can for *I love you*.

Oscar gives Kip a motivational talk and then a running start. Miraculously he flies over the top of us, and the three of us lie there for a couple more beats than we need to before standing up because it feels like old times. When we were close and comfortable with one another.

eighteen

Now

I play my music on shuffle in the common room and think about how when internet trolls are exposed, they're not always the inadequate, obsessive loners that people expect. Something brushes my shoulder, and I turn with a start to see Kerry standing there with Alice, trying to get my attention. I pull out an earphone.

"You want to come into the village with us and Dani?" says Kerry. "We're going to check out the shop."

I pull an I'm-not-sure face. "Come on," she says. "It's stopped raining, and it's free time now. We've heard they sell sweets in jars, like in old-fashioned sweet shops."

Up the other end of the room, Danielle has found a

remote control and is flicking through the TV channels.

"All right," I say, though I know Kerry's probably only inviting me because she feels sorry for me having my pool phobia so publicly blabbed. "Thanks." I walk with her and Alice towards our rooms to fetch some money. Danielle catches us up and doesn't seem bothered either way when Kerry announces I'm coming into the village with them.

"See you two in the reception building in ten minutes," says Alice as she and Kerry veer off towards their accommodation block.

Danielle's mobile rings as she pushes open the glass entry door to our block. She looks at the screen. "What d'you want now, Dad?" she mutters, but when she answers the call, her voice is far sunnier: "Hi, Dad! What's up?" She indicates for me to carry on while she wanders back outside.

I place my phone on my chest of drawers and select a thick-ish shirt to wear over my T-shirt for warmth. Tartan. Something to rival Brandon's shirt collection.

As I fish out some money from my purse to take with me, my phone pings. I lunge at it.

LUISA: I want you to be happy but I'm upset with you.

I didn't save you. That's my first thought. Until I pull myself together. Someone either knows what happened last summer, or they've found out from the internet. It wouldn't be difficult to work out from newspaper articles about Luisa's death that I was the "unnamed teenager in the property at the time of the incident who was treated for shock at the scene." Perhaps I made things worse with my You Don't Scare Me reply. Is the person pretending to be Luisa trying to provoke a reaction for the fun of it, or is there menace in their message?

I yank open the room door and look for Danielle through the entry door. She's still on the phone, pacing slowly up and down on the grass outside. She sees me and tips her head up and down to say to me *All right, all right. I'm coming.*

"Relax," she says when she comes back into the room. "We've got loads of time. Kerry and Alice won't go without us."

I could find a reason to go home and escape this, or at least feel safer. It would be like hiding though, and I'm not doing that. I tuck my phone into my shirt pocket, next to my money, and wait for Danielle to find her purse and change her shoes.

The village shop is disappointing. There are three large jars, containing chipped sherbet lemons, strawberry toffee bonbons and jelly beans, and that's their entire old-fashioned sweet selection. Alice buys a small paper bag's worth of jelly beans. It costs her three times as much as if she'd bought them in plastic packaging and she receives a disproportionate amount of green ones. The rest of us choose an assortment of chocolate bars and flip through the magazines until we're told if we look any longer, we'll have to buy one, so we pay for the chocolate and plonk ourselves on the bench up the road, next to a grey stone cross. The village war memorial. A few cars hurtle past us and a white cat climbs a tree on the other side of the road.

"Not a lot happens in this village, does it?" says Kerry.

Danielle shrugs. "Just cos you can't see it, doesn't mean it's not happening."

Alice hands round her jelly beans, telling us to close our eyes and guess what flavour we've picked. We're not making much noise but an old man who's shuffling towards the shop stops to lean on his stick and stare at us.

"Old people annoy me," says Danielle when he's moved off. "I hate that they've survived beyond forty-four years old." She wanders up to the stone cross, stands on the first step of it and reads out a few names. "The Truss family were hit hard." She jumps down. "Who wants to play that game where you see how long you can lie in the middle of the road for?"

Kerry laughs. "Dani, you're a nutter. You haven't even been drinking."

"All right. I'll go first," says Danielle. She smooths out the front of her T-shirt and lies down on the black tarmac in front of the stone cross, her hands under her head. "This road's really warm," she says.

I stop eating my Twix. Cars can come from three directions, round two blind corners or from the junction next to the war memorial. The three of us on the bench look at one another.

"I can hear something coming," says Alice.

"No, you can't," says Danielle.

I stand up, my ears straining. Sweat gathers under my arms. A high-pitched whir of machinery comes and goes. There's something else now. A rattling noise.

"Get up, Dani!" says Kerry.

"It's a trailer," says Alice, moving away from us towards the direction she thinks it's coming from. A few seconds later a Land Rover appears, coming towards us from the side road next to the memorial, a low trailer bouncing along behind it.

My mouth is too dry to shout, but I rush forward to Danielle, to pull her up. She's on her feet, pushing me away. "Calm down, Skye. No need to panic."

The driver of the Land Rover barely looks at us as he turns left, away from us.

"OK, I'll have one more go," says Danielle. She sits down on the road.

"Hang on," says Alice. Kerry is saying something too. We're all in the road.

There's definitely a vehicle coming, this time from the right, and it's fast.

"Move!" I shout, and we stagger back into the grassy verge together as a white van emerges from the tunnel of leafy trees. It slows down past us, as I shriek and cling on to Alice to avoid sliding further down into a boggy ditch, but picks up speed again at the memorial.

"Did you see the driver's face?" laughs Danielle. Her eyes are shining. "We really made him jump."

nineteen

Fay has saved me a place next to her for dinner. "Where've you been?" she asks. "I couldn't find you earlier."

"The village," I say. "Then Danielle and I went to Alice and Kerry's room. We played cards and Danielle set up an online profile for Kerry on a dating website. How about you?"

"I had the counselling... Then I couldn't find you or Joe, so I went exploring."

I twist spaghetti with my fork as Fay tells me she walked round the edge of the grounds and found Joe jogging round the lake. She and Joe sat near the lake and had a Deep Meaningful Conversation.

"He gets me," she says. "He understands what I've been through. He was inspirational, actually."

Inspirational? Hmm. I reach for my napkin to wipe sauce off my chin.

"We talked about Kyra too. He's had a tough day today with it being her birthday. Did you know, he helps out on websites for teenagers who feel depressed? He should be a proper counsellor." She looks down the table to where Joe is talking loudly about surfing. "He's a very spiritual person when you get to know him."

"You don't find him a bit. . ." I struggle to find the right word. "Pushy?"

"He has strong opinions, but I like that. He's sure of himself. Like my dad was. My dad loved coming up with new theories about things."

For some reason she's talking about religion now, and I filter her voice out as I wrestle with my spaghetti.

"Oh! I forgot to say," says Fay in a higher pitch. "I've sorted out a team for tonight's quiz. It's you, me and Joe."

"Oh?"

"Pippa needed the names of the teams for her spreadsheet. We're called Quiz Whiz."

Great.

It's an inter-group activity. Everyone is in a team apart from a couple of leftover people who are helping to hand out paper and pens. That's the role I'd prefer to sitting here in a team with Fay, who's sitting very straight, and Joe, who's practically horizontal, one knee up against the table and his body leaning back against the chair.

"You're going to have to switch that off in a minute," Joe says to me, eyeing my phone like a disapproving teacher. "Or we'll be disqualified."

"I know," I say, and carry on flipping through my social media sites. Waiting for Fake Luisa to get in touch. I want him or her to trip up and say something that will identify themselves.

Joe moves his knee, and without warning he's right up close to me. "What's so interesting?" His leg touches mine, and I shoot back on my seat, moving my leg and phone out of his way.

I check to see if Fay's noticed, but she's watching the paper and pens being handed out.

"Nothing," I say. If I made a comment about him invading my personal space, he'd bounce it back at me, saying I was uptight.

"Mobile phones. I hate them," says Joe. "I have to have one, but I hate them."

He must have sat through a similar amount of how-to-be-appropriate-with-technology talks at school as I have. I can't be bothered to enter the debate. In fact I don't need to because Joe's off on a rant about people spending more time on their phone than talking to each other. I almost laugh out loud; I'd rather be on my phone than hearing what he's got to say.

One pen and several sheets of paper are placed on our table. Fay sweeps them towards her. I turn off my phone, the quiz begins and my mind works fast, just not on the right questions. Why would someone pretend to be Luisa? Did they hack into MessageHound and randomly stumble on to Luisa's and my private chat, or are they targeting me specifically? They only messaged me back when I sent that first message, but how long have they had access to the account for?

I feel watched.

"D'you know that one?" asks Joe.

"What?" I ask. So far I've sat and looked on as Fay's written down the answers with minimal consultation with Joe.

"Name the first names of the members of the group ABBA."

"Clue's in the name," I say. "It's why they were called ABBA: Agnetha, Björn, Benny and Anni-Frid. My mum's a fan."

"Yeah, that's right," says Joe, as if he knew it all along and he was making me earn my keep on the team.

As soon as it's over and Pippa has collected the answer sheets, I turn on my phone. It pings immediately.

"If you're checking the answers," says Fay, "I wasn't one hundred per cent sure about the baby penguin question. If they're chicks or fledglings?"

"I'm not," I say. "Sorry. I'll be back in a minute." I stand up and move away to the other end of the room, near where Pippa and two instructors are settling down to mark the quiz sheets.

LUISA: That tartan shirt suits you.

I dart my eyes round the hall. Turn a full circle, my body on hyper-alert. It was always unlikely that the person behind the messages was a random stranger, but now I know for sure. It's someone who knows exactly who I am.

This has gone too far.

Joe wanders up with a bottle of water in his hands. He takes a swig from it and smacks his lips. "You'd be much happier if you weren't so angry all the time," he says.

Is it him?

"Where's your phone?" I ask.

"Calm down. You're very aggressive." He holds his hands up. One's holding the water bottle, the other the lid. "I'm not like you. My phone isn't surgically attached to me. It's back in my room."

He could be lying. His phone could be hidden somewhere back at the table, under a jumper or in a bag of some sort. "Please leave me alone." I turn away from him and busy myself with the baby penguin question.

"We're all mixed up on this holiday, but you – you're a league apart," says Joe softly. His eyes scare me a little with their intensity.

"You think so?" I try to appear unruffled, to show him that I can brush his nasty remarks away easily. "How very nearly interesting."

I click on a penguin website. The young are usually called chicks, but they can be called fledglings. Fay will be happy; she wrote down fledglings. I look up. Fay's watching Joe come back to the table, her face anxious. Did she have a phone on her earlier? I study the room. Danielle and Brandon are both on their phones, as are Kerry and Alice, and some of the Reds and Blues.

I've been wearing this shirt all afternoon and evening. The person messaging me could be anyone in this room.

We're told to regroup in our teams for the results. Under the table, Fay's legs are trembling. When she sees I've noticed, she places a hand on each of her thighs to still them. Everyone eventually quieten downs as Pippa holds up the prizes: bars of chocolate and the pens with *Have an adventure with us* stamped on them that you can buy in reception for £1.99, and three tacky trophies.

"We'll announce the winning teams in reverse order. In third place, team Giant Cookie. . ." She reads out three names and we clap while those people come up to receive their chocolate. "In second place, Quiz Whiz. . ." I turn to Fay. Her head is bowed. She's gutted we didn't come first.

"We get the pens!" I say. "Come on, Fay. You did brilliantly."

Joe murmurs in her ear and massages her shoulder to encourage her to go up. I'm embarrassed to be associated with the pair of them, so I stand up first and collect the pen that I answered one question for. We get huge applause. Of course – we're Yellows, the group the others feel sorry for. The three of us have to pose for a photo. We're told to lean in close to one another, hold our pens up and say "prizewinners". I hope I never have to see a copy of it.

The team that comes first are Reds. They don't look surprised to have won. Fay can hardly bear to look at them.

A man with a moustache who appears to be the Reds' leader urges us all to mingle for the next couple of hours. He points out the cans of drink on the counter where the breakfast cereals usually are and says any moment now there'll be music when they work out how to switch on the music system. "Please socialize, make friends, and we'll see you all back here tomorrow evening for the disco."

The room reverts to chatter, but the three of us sit for a moment in silence. A couple of Blues walk behind my chair and I hear one whisper to the other that he's heard Yellow Group are orphans.

I stand. "I'll see you later," I say, and I leave Fay and Joe to each other.

I sit outside on the fire-escape steps, at the back of the dining hall with a supermarket own brand of orange soda. I know I shouldn't engage with whoever it is who's turned the messaging into a form of stalking, but I want to sound strong and in control.

SKYE: Tell me why you're stalking me.

I take a mouthful of orange soda, and the tingling fizz of it is still on the roof my mouth when a reply comes back.

LUISA: I'm not stalking you. We're not enemies.

It would have been better to be sitting in the hall, able to look round and see who was messaging.

"Hi." Brandon's standing at the corner of the building. He made me jump. "I wondered where you'd gone." He walks up to the fire escape. "Congratulations, by the way, on coming second." He holds up his can of lemonade in acknowledgement.

"Thanks," I say, "but I only answered the question about ABBA."

"Are you OK if I sit down? The music choice in the dining room is a little . . . not my taste."

I switch my phone screen off. "What d'you know about MessageHound?" I ask. I watch his face closely when I say MessageHound. It sort of scrunches up with the effort of remembering. Or the pretence of remembering. It's ironic that I accused him of stalking me when we were about to go orienteering, just because he kept choosing the same activities as me, whereas now I genuinely am being stalked.

"Err, it's been around for ages and hardly anyone uses it any more. Why?"

"I'm on a group chat and it's been hacked," I say. "I want to find the hacker."

"Why bother?" asks Brandon. "Just get everyone to change their passwords, or set up a new chat."

"Yes, but. . ." I hesitate. I watch him get comfortable on the step below mine. Our heads are almost the same height now. I'd like to touch his face, trace a finger along his cheekbones, but I can't let myself get too close to him until I know for sure that he's not behind the messages.

"My brother knew loads about hacking," he says.

"What about you?" I ask.

"Nah. I'm into animation. We both were, me and my brother. He wanted to do film studies at uni." He drains the last of the drink from his can, and pushes inwards with his thumb all the way round the top. I can tell this conversation is costing him effort. "He made a series of four video clips for me, and when he knew he didn't have much time left, he programmed his email to send them to me once a month. The first one arrived when he was still alive but he couldn't speak, and the others came after he'd died. It was freaky."

So he's experienced a bit of what I have. "Like messages from a dead person?"

Brandon nods. "He was obsessed with the idea of creating virtual avatars for dead people. There are companies already doing it, using data from emails, photos, social media – anything digital."

"But after you got over the freakiness, did you like getting them?"

"Yeah." He places the can in between his Converse. "I did. Mum got hysterical though. Each time one came through she wanted to watch it straight away, but then she'd break down within the first second. Dad was still living with us then. He had them backed up all over the place so they couldn't be lost."

"D'you ever watch them now?"

"Sometimes. When I can't remember the sound of his voice."

There's a ping from my phone. I force myself to ignore it, but I sag inside with relief. Brandon can't be behind the messages because he's right here with me. I ask him about his blog and I feel bad because I only half concentrate as he tells me what makes the perfect trailer for a film or book. How the things that are left out can be more important than what goes in. About lasting impressions.

When his talk dries up, he says, "Want to go for a walk?"

Badly, yes. So much that I'm tingling without having had any soda since Brandon found me. But I need to know what that new message says. I hesitate too long and he clears his throat and says, "You know, I think I'll wander back in and see what the others are up to."

He picks up the can and turns away, avoiding any more eye contact. I watch him go, aware of a hollow feeling in my stomach. As soon as I can no longer see him, I touch the icon like the MessageHound addict that I've become. I hate myself. I don't even care what this message says any more.

LUISA: Don't tell anyone about this.

Is this a threat? My limbs shake uncontrollably from fear but I manage to stand, and walk slowly towards my accommodation, vigilant of everything around me.

Brandon's talk of avatars makes me glad there isn't

any film footage on the app in case my stalker could manipulate it into something really creepy. All at once, the part of the conversation about Brandon's brother programming his email to send his video clips comes back to me. I find the settings option in the MessageHound app. About halfway down are the words *Schedule Message*. I never knew that option existed. Joe could have written the messages earlier in the evening and scheduled them to send later. So could Brandon or anyone else. I see how easily a person could reply directly to my messages sometimes, and schedule other things in between. That way, they could, if they wanted, make sure they're with me when I receive a message, and get a kick from my reaction. I withdraw my hands and my phone into the sleeves of my tartan shirt and hug myself tight.

twenty

SKYE: Why would I take any notice of you?

I schedule it to be sent at three a.m. for the hell of it, and when I wake at seven a.m. there's no reply yet.

It's unsettling to wake up in a place where you're not sure who to trust. The list of suspects has been circulating in my head all night: Joe, Danielle, Brandon, Fay, Alice, Kerry. Plus the rest of the Yellows, and all the Reds and Blues, except these messages seem personal. But anybody here could be aware of Luisa's death, or connected to her in some way without me knowing.

When Fay comes out of the bathroom and asks why I haven't got up for breakfast, I tell her I'm too tired, and pull the duvet halfway over my head. I'm not lying about the tiredness, but I'm not ready to face the day and my stalker yet either.

Fay doesn't bother to ask Danielle, who's either still asleep or pretending to be. "Are you sure, Skye?"

"Yeah," I say. "Irony in action – you going for breakfast, me staying in bed."

"Joe says I should eat breakfast."

"Good for Joe," I say, and jerk the duvet closed at the top, over my head, for a few moments until she goes.

Later, when Danielle goes into the bathroom, I see her phone peeking out from under her pillow. It makes a vibrate noise and I listen to check that she's in the shower before I leap across and lift the pillow to see what's on the screen.

There's an image of an album cover I don't recognize, probably because I haven't reached the required level of cool, and overlaying that is a text from someone called Chazza:

How are the wacko room-mates?

I'm not sure what I was hoping to find on Danielle's phone, but it wasn't that. No doubt Danielle's providing a running commentary about Fay and me to her mates. Nice.

I dart back into my duvet nest. Is Danielle playing with me on MessageHound because she thinks I'm a wacko? Easily wound up? I shouldn't have told her about Luisa and our chat group the night she gave me the sleeping pill.

"Paintballing today," says Danielle when she comes out of the bathroom. "Excellent. I like a fight."

After breakfast, Fay returns to the room and says she's not doing paintballing because she did it once and was hit by a load of paintballs.

"Isn't that the whole point of paintball?" I ask.

"I was bruised for months," she says. "I spoke to Pippa at breakfast and she says it's fine for me to stay here and sit on the patio outside the games room." She takes an enormous book out of her suitcase. A chemistry textbook.

All of us Yellows except Fay wait in the reception building with an instructor for the minibus to take us to the paintball centre. I study a wildlife poster and reflect on the fact that the photo of the jaunty fox looks nothing like the mangy animals that cruise the residential streets where I now live. Danielle is in a huddle with Alice and Kerry. Joe is having an earnest discussion with Henry, and Brandon is laughing with his room-mate Jack. I don't blame Brandon for wanting to hang out with him rather than me after I gave him the cold shoulder yesterday evening. It's OK though; I have a poster to look at.

My phone pings as I study the photo of a strange crested bird. There's a familiar thump in my stomach when I see Luisa's name and read her imposter's message.

LUISA: It's nice to talk when times are tough.

I look around me but no one has their phones out. I

can't tell if it's a scheduled message or not, but at least it's softer in tone.

I'm going to keep going with this weirdness until my stalker trips up. There are two days left at Morley Hill and I want to find out who's doing this before I leave. I take a breath and type:

SKYE: What d'you want to talk about?

I send and look up, waiting to see if anyone reaches for their phone after hearing an alert or feeling it vibrate. No one does.

On the minibus, Brandon has the choice of sitting next to me, but he walks past and plonks himself on the back seat. Danielle sits next to me because she wants to be near Alice and Kerry, who are sitting on the two seats in the opposite row. As soon as the minibus is moving, she undoes her seat belt and swivels her legs round into the aisle.

Danielle is talking to Kerry and Alice about dumb ways to die. They list the people they've heard of who have slipped off cliffs, electrocuted or accidentally stabbed themselves, and I try not to listen because it panics me when I think about how many ways there are to die. "You've got to have heard that song," says Danielle. "'Dumb Ways to Die'. It's Australian. My friend and I learned all the words and performed it at a talent show one year. I'll find it for you. Hang on." She finds her phone in her pocket and switches it on. "Rubbish signal," she says. "Give me a moment." She hums. "Okaaay. Text message from my dad. He's so effing hopeless. He can't remember where we keep the light bulbs."

I look back at my phone and read through Mum's texts from this morning. She's not hopeless. She's efficient and organized. But her need for everything to turn out well is exhausting. I send a perky text back – the sort she likes. *All good.* ☺ *Paintballing this morning.* The MessageHound dog's tail wags and I open the message as fast as I can.

LUISA: What d'you think of Moorly Hill?

A super-quick answer to my question that I sent just minutes ago. The high-pitched noise I make in my throat embarrasses me, but Danielle doesn't turn round. Did she have time in those seconds when she was replying to her dad's text and searching on the internet for the song to bat back that answer? I lean across and look at her phone, and catch sight of a colourful animation that she and the others are laughing at.

Unbuckling my seat belt, I semi-stand to look round the minibus. Joe's at the front of the bus next to the instructor. I can't see his hands but he's looking straight ahead. On the back seat, Brandon is talking to Jack. Both Joe and Brandon would have had time to have sent a quick message and put their phones away.

Morley is spelled wrong. Is that because the person was typing quickly or because they're a bad speller? I can more or less strike Fay off the list of suspects. She's a perfectionist, the type to reread a message before sending it. Certainly a message like this.

We drive into a vast wooded area with no houses in sight. When the minibus stops, I'm half-expecting to be handed a bow and arrow and be injected with a tracker. I'm given black overalls, helmet, goggles and gloves from a guy called Dave, and told to put any valuables including phones into a locker, before queuing up for a gun and paintballs. I check my phone one last time before placing it in my locker. Another text from Mum. *Oscar and I are baking a cake!*

The Blues arrived earlier on a coach. They're inside the first part of the enclosure, so bored with waiting for us that they're not even pretending to shoot each other and are sitting in the dirt, up against the fence. Dave makes everyone do a couple of minutes of warm-up exercises, splits us into random groups, and dishes out four sets of bibs for team colours.

The first game is a simple eliminate-the-opposition game — as soon as a player's hit, they have to leave the shooting area, and the team with the last person standing wins. I shoot two people in quick succession, and the surge of adrenaline it brings loosens my limbs and makes me feel strong and determined. My team doesn't win but I'm one of the last few people to be shot.

Dave shows us into a picnic area to wait for the next game while another group finish. It's more inner-city wasteland than woodland picnic spot. There are several lopsided picnic tables that have initials carved into them, a few tufts of grass and masses of fag ends. Three white plastic chairs on their sides are dotted round the site, as if they blew over in the winter and have become part of the landscape.

The Blues rush to the picnic tables but leave one for us, like priority seating on a bus. For the elderly, disabled, pregnant or Yellow.

Danielle picks up a chair, hitches up the legs of her trousers and flops down. "That was tough. I'm ready to quit now."

"Winners never quit and quitters never win," says Joe.

"Yeah, yeah. Thanks for the pep talk," says Danielle. "In case you hadn't noticed, I'm not even on your team."

Joe walks over to the remaining picnic table and sits on top of it, his feet on the bench part. Literally sitting himself above everyone else. "Anyone here want to discuss the best paintballing tactics?" he asks. "There's quite a bit of interesting psychology to it."

"Discuss?" I say. "I thought you preferred telling people what to do."

Henry laughs. "Go on then, Joe. What's the best strategy?"

"Don't rush in. Watch and wait. Then watch and wait some more."

"Very profound," I say.

Dave shouts, "Time to rehydrate, guys!" He explains the next game. Two teams play at a time and each has to capture their opponents' flag, which flies from the top of their wooden fort.

We follow Dave into the urban zone, which, as well as two forts, has all sorts of wrecked stuff as part of the scene, including a burned-out car. This game is less manic and more stealthy. My team work well together and make it to the next round.

The final game starts slowly. I slither on the ground for the first few minutes, wriggling past the cars to reach a shack that's been made out of an old bus shelter and some metal panels.

Brandon and Kerry – who are also in my team – manage to scoot across open land to safety behind a wall of dustbins, a little bit closer to the opposition's fort, and everything goes eerily quiet for a few seconds while no one else moves.

Shouting and shooting erupt again and I peek out of the narrow gap in the metal panels to see that a Blue member of our team has come out of nowhere and eliminated the two people patrolling the fort. He scales the building in several quick movements while the other side frantically take aim. It's a total fluke that he isn't hit. He lifts the flag from its holder and waves it triumphantly.

Game over. We've won.

I walk out of the shelter and I'm grabbed from behind. An arm locks itself across my neck as my stomach drops. Prevented from being able to walk upright, I stagger backwards, lose my footing and am dragged.

Panic surges upwards like vomit.

"I've got a hostage," shouts my assailant. It's Joe. "I'll swap her for the flag."

"Nice try," says someone. I can't see because my head has been yanked back. Why isn't anyone stopping him?

"Get off me," I say, kicking backwards. My kicks don't connect with anything, so I wriggle as hard as I can. The grip round my neck tightens and I'm gut-squeezed-scared that I won't be able to breathe. That I'm seconds away from passing out.

"OK. That's enough. Let her go," says Dave.

"Say please." It's a whisper in my ear. I can visualize now how Joe's standing. For a couple of seconds I stop resisting; then I swiftly elbow him as hard as I can in the area I hope is his groin.

"Bitch." He releases me, lurches away towards one of his team members.

"You have a problem," I shout. "Keep away from me."

He straightens up and strolls off, shaking his head. I sit down on a recycling bin. Shaky and hot.

"Gather round, people," shouts Dave. He waves me over.

I wait until the last possible moment to walk up. Dave says, "I know losing can be tough. I know that some of you get pumped up when playing paintball, but let's keep things cool, yeah? You –" he points to Joe "– you need to apologize to this girl for taking things too far back there."

"Really? I was only fooling about, but sure." Joe holds his hand up in a wave. "Sorry if you took it the wrong way."

I don't reply. I don't even nod. Dave says, "Solid. I don't

want to see that sort of behaviour again. Now it's time for lunch."

"What did Joe do?" asks Brandon, appearing next to me as we're herded towards a mobile catering van that's parked at the entrance to the centre. "Did he hurt you?"

"Took me as a hostage. Wanted me to beg for my release." I rub my neck where his arm was pressing against me. "I don't know if he did it because I challenged him earlier."

"He's a bad loser," says Brandon.

We're each handed a vivid green drink and a polystyrene box filled with chips, battered fish and a few sachets of ketchup, which we have to eat in the picnic area. Most Yellows crush on to the picnic table, four a side. Joe's among them. I hear him talk loudly about raw foods and how he usually tries to eat a macrobiotic diet, whatever that is. He doesn't glance in my direction at all.

Brandon joins Jack and Nate, who are sitting cross-legged on the ground, and I follow. After what's happened, I don't want to sit anywhere near Joe. The chips are pale and flabby, and the battered fish sits in a pool of oil. I close up the box again.

"Food's gross, isn't it?" says Jack, as he shoves a giant-size chip into his mouth in one go. "Don't blame you for not eating it."

It's not just the grossness of the food. I'm still in shock. Humiliated. I hate to think what Joe would be like as a boyfriend. Outward charm and inner fury. Over-dominating. I shudder as I remember his insistent, creeping hands on my skin. His keenness to know everything about me. And I told him most of it, like a fool, on day one.

"I'm going to the lockers to check my phone," I say to the boys. "If Dave asks, tell him I've gone to the toilet."

"What's up? You kept checking it on the minibus," says Brandon.

Why was he watching me on the minibus? And what's it to him anyway?

"Nothing..." I stand up. "My mum's being stressy, that's all."

My phone is warm as a pebble from being inside the locker in the heat. I walk away from the stinking toilet block and sit on a pile of discarded wood. No one's in sight, yet I constantly look round as I switch on my phone and check that last misspelled message again. *What d'you think of Moorly Hill?*

The wood, or the damp area around it, smells rotten and unpleasant, but it's a marginal improvement on the toilets and I have a signal on my phone, which is what I need to find out more about Joe. A Google search isn't going to tell me if he's the person sending the messages, but it might explain his unhinged behaviour.

He's a member of a climbing club, and he's won a surfing competition in Cornwall. He has tight privacy settings on his social media. Everything else I find turns out to be about other Joes with the same surname.

I squeeze my eyes together. *Think. Think.* What was the name of Joe's ex-girlfriend? Something beginning with K... Kate, Kylie. *Kyra.* I don't remember the town she came from or anything else about her. I search under her first name, *suicide* and *bullying*. The phone takes a while to load the page of top results. I scan it and don't see anything that jumps out as being anything to do with Joe's ex-girlfriend. I go to the next page, and the next. Has he fabricated it? Changed the details? Everyone on this holiday has been referred by school or a counsellor or some professional. He can't have made the whole thing up.

Local Girl Took Own Life Because of Bullies.

When I click on the link and see the photo, I recognize Joe's Kyra. She's wearing school uniform and her hair's tied up. Smiling one of those self-conscious no-teeth smiles for the school photographer.

I don't know what I'm hoping to find. I read through the article. Kyra lived with her mum and older brother. She took an overdose of her grandad's painkillers... It emerged after her death that she'd taken a photo of herself naked and sent it to a boy at school, who'd forwarded it on, and it had gone viral in the area.

If Kyra was going out with Joe at the time, why did she send that boy a naked photo of herself?

There's a quote from her mum. *"The family's devastated. Kyra left a note telling us how ashamed she was, but she had nothing to be ashamed of."*

Kyra's headmaster is also quoted saying she was a hard-working, well-liked student, and he sends the family his deepest sympathy.

The article ends with information about the funeral, a "small family ceremony" followed by a memorial service two months later on October twenty-fourth "on what would have been Kyra's sixteenth birthday."

I reread the sentence. Joe said Kyra's sixteenth birthday would have been yesterday. I think back to his tearless performance at breakfast. What was all that about? Did the idea of a birthday come to him because it had been Brandon's the day before?

I search for other articles, trying other keywords from details I've got from the first one. There's a much shorter one, printed the day after the memorial service. I enlarge the accompanying photo as much as I can. The caption reads *Kyra's family and friends celebrate her life*. It shows a group of people going into a church, heads slightly down, in dark coats and scarves. I spot Joe straight away. He's being helped along by a girl either side who have linked their arms through his.

Attention. He likes the attention. And he's a good liar.

twenty-one

As soon as I'm back in our room at Morley Hill, I grab the first shower. Danielle is furious but I ignore her swearing, and drown out the loud repetitive dance tracks that she plays on her portable speakers with the sound of running water. I've left my phone on the side of the sink, so I can glance at it every so often to see if the screen's lit up from receiving a message because I know I won't hear the alert.

Fay comes back to the room after I've changed into shorts and T-shirt, while I'm rootling through my suitcase for a disco outfit for tonight. I find the one dress I packed. It's black, sleeveless and plain. It probably doesn't look as good on me as it used to. When I was slimmer, fitter, different. I drape it over the top of my suitcase so it doesn't become any more creased than it already is.

"How was paintballing?" asks Fay as she drops her textbook on her bed.

"OK until Joe took me hostage, allegedly as a joke."

"Really? He wouldn't be doing it to be mean. He's anti-violence of any sort."

"I looked up his girlfriend online." I want Fay to see what Joe's really like. "There was a local newspaper article. It said Kyra's birthday was in October. Not July."

Fay frowns. "They must have got it wrong. You can't trust newspapers to get their facts right."

"But it said the family chose the date of the memorial service especially because it would have been her sixteenth birthday. That would be hard to get wrong, wouldn't it?"

"There'll be an explanation." Fay's blinking goes into overtime. "I'll ask him. He'll tell me straight. I know he will."

That wasn't what I was after. I was going to tackle him myself, but if she wants to do it, that's fine. There's an alert from my phone, the one that means I have a text. I double-check the screen. Mum.

Fay sits cross-legged on her bed, then draws her knees up. It looks like a yoga position, or one of those challenges to see how small you can make your body. I spot her revolting toy rabbit in the bend of one elbow. Is she ... she can't be ... *sniffing* her rabbit?

If she was Oscar's age, I'd sit beside her and tell her

that I'm sorry I upset her by hating on Joe when I know how much she likes him. But I did it to warn her, because despite her being so annoying there are aspects of her that I like, traits I understand. She thinks about stuff more deeply than most people, but I see how guilt exhausts her and sets her apart. How eating and achievements are no longer simple things for her.

"How was the chemistry?" I ask from my bed, on the other side of the room. The sides of the textbook are grey from being handled so often and there are neon Post-it markers sticking out in three directions.

"Couldn't concentrate. I was thinking about my dad and the crash. Sometimes I feel so ashamed I can't concentrate on anything else."

"That must be horrible." I'm too much of a coward to say "I know how it feels." I lie back against the pillow, clutching my phone.

"What if I hadn't had the argument? What if I'd never got in the car? Said I'd skip my flute lesson, or that I'd get the bus?" If her blinking gets any faster she'll have some sort of strobe–effect–induced fit. "I was angry because he wouldn't leave when I wanted him to. He wouldn't finish his phone call to his colleague." She clutches her head, the rabbit dropping into her lap.

She isn't aware how much I identify with what she's saying. How deeply the *what if*s, the *if only*s and *why didn't I*s haunt me too, but I can't be as open with her as she is with me.

The bathroom door swings open so wide that it bangs against the wall. Danielle stands with her hand on her hips in her kimono-style dressing gown. "Skye, did you use my conditioner?"

"Er, yes. Sorry. I used mine up."

"You should have asked." Danielle does a double-take at Fay. "What's the matter with you?"

"Nothing," says Fay. She lifts her head. "Thinking about things."

"Don't think too hard. It's bad for you." Danielle reaches for her hairbrush on her chest of drawers. "God, I dread to think how much of a fail this disco tonight's going to be. But the upside is I might get some classic awkward moments on camera." She holds up her phone. I wish she'd stop with the filming, but if anyone complains Pippa might impose a phone ban and I couldn't handle that.

I ignore her and inspect the scab on my knee. "By the way," says Fay. "Pippa asked me to remind you about the talk on developing resilience in half an hour."

Resilience sounds like a disease.

"Not my thing," I say.

Danielle's music suddenly blares out through her speakers.

"I've got a headache," says Fay. "Please could you put your earphones in."

When Danielle has reluctantly redirected her music through her earphones and Fay has rolled over towards the window to read more of her textbook, I turn my attention to my phone.

There are photos all over social media of people's holidays. Swimming pools. Barbecues. Crazy ice creams. Boats. Smiling faces. Annika is in Cyprus with her family. She's posted a photo of her dad's epic belly flop into the pool. It's a proper-size pool. It has to be. Annika's training out there. Keeping up with her swim schedule. Most of the outfits she's wearing in the photos are clothes I've never seen her in before. They represent all the shopping trips that I wasn't there for.

As soon as Fay leaves for the talk and Danielle disappears to make a private phone call, I decide to Google everybody else in Yellow Group whose surname I can remember from the sign-up sheets.

Ironically for someone so willing to invade other people's privacy, Danielle is almost totally anonymous online apart from a mention in one article. She was nominated for an award at a young carers' association, for looking after her wheelchair-bound dad, and her mother, before she died of cancer of the spleen. It doesn't mean she hasn't hacked into MessageHound. I don't find anything that allows me to eliminate or flag up anyone else either.

I allow myself a quick scroll through the MessageHound photos. A moment of pretending that everything is as it used to be and Luisa is at the other end of the messages. I find a photo of her foot, taken to show me a bruise on it from someone treading on it at a party. I know it's from last summer because of her red and pink toenails. My eyes switch to my own pink and red toenails. The nail varnish is chipped on a couple of nails. I should probably paint them a different colour, and that thought brings with it a rush of sadness.

By the time it comes to the evening, I'm not certain I can face a disco with a load of holiday camp kids who I don't know and a few I barely know. And Joe. The alternative, however, is to hang out in the room with Fay, who says she doesn't want to go because she hates loud music and is tired.

"You should try it for a bit," I say, as much to myself as to her. "You can always come back if you hate it. It's not as if you have to wait for a bus or a parent to come and pick you up, is it?" I grasp my dress at the waist and twist the fabric round me to see how tight it's got. It's more of a clinging than skimming situation.

"Joe's going, isn't he?" says Danielle. "I'd have thought that was a good enough reason for you." She checks her heavy eye make-up in her little mirror, and I wonder who's looking after her dad back home. If she trusts the person to do a good job.

My phone pings.

"That high-pitched noise is irritating," says Danielle. "Can't you change it to a duck quack or something?"

I look at her. Has she scheduled this message? I'm itching to open it, but I don't want to do it in front of her.

Fay pushes her feet into some glittery ballet-pump shoes that have an elastic strap across the foot. The type that bridesmaids wear. Ten-year-old bridesmaids. "I'm ready," she says, the mention of Joe having clearly changed her mind.

"You go on," I say. "I need to text my mum back."

"I don't mind waiting," says Fay.

"I'm going," says Danielle. "See you." She pushes past me and shoots off.

Fay hovers near her bed, and I open the message, concentrating on keeping my face as emotionless as I can.

LUISA: Don't forget.

"Skye? Skye – is everything all right with your mum?"

"What?" I see Fay coming over, frowning with concern. "Oh. No. It's fine. I'm fine. Let's go."

Don't forget ... Luisa? Or something else? Two small, confusing words that make me shiver as I walk along the path with Fay in the humid evening.

Some effort has been put into making the main dining hall look less of a canteen and more of a disco venue, with black curtains at the windows, lights and a dangling mirrored ball. There's a proper DJ, or at least a live person, doing the music. Nobody's dancing yet, but the place is full. In the gloom, I can see that the tables round the hall are all taken.

Fay clutches my arm as we walk in, and whispers, "Don't leave me, will you?"

"No, don't worry," I say, although my heart sinks a little.

All the Yellows are sitting at the same table. Danielle's nabbed the last seat, next to Brandon. Joe's talking to Alice, offering advice, no doubt, and keeping up his image of Mr Nice Guy.

"Wait." I hold Fay back from walking towards the table. "There aren't any more chairs there. Let's sit somewhere else."

"Where?" asks Fay.

We gaze round, and Fay says, "Look," and I see that Brandon is waving us over. Before I can say anything, Fay is halfway across the hall.

Keep breathing. In through the nose, out through the mouth.

"Here, Skye!" Brandon offers me half his seat. Alice moves and perches on Kerry's lap, and Fay sits on the vacated seat, even though it would make much more sense for Fay to sit on someone's lap since she's by far the lightest person here. Joe moves his chair closer to hers. "How are you feeling?" I hear him murmur.

I inch in beside Brandon, trying to judge how far my bum will overhang. He smells of a deodorant that's more subtle than your average boy's. He's wearing jeans, and a shirt that's got a black-and-white photographic print of flowers on it.

"The shirt was a present," he says when he sees me giving it the once-over. "Not my usual style."

*

Everyone's joking about the terrible music. Jack rolls some tubes of Pringles on the table, and Brandon shows us how to slot the crisps together to make a big ring. When we've taken photos, someone prods it, and the crisps scatter, some of them skimming into people's laps, some off the table on to the floor. Danielle produces a bottle of vodka from her bag, swigs from it, and hands it to Kerry. "Pass it round." The music's improved and a couple of people go to dance, then a couple more. I move across to sit on a vacant seat.

"D'you like dancing?" asks Brandon. He has to shout a little so I can hear.

I wobble my hand. It means: *Sort of. Depends.* I glance across at Fay and she catches my eye. She nods. It means *I'm OK here with Joe. Off you go.*

"Come on!" Brandon mouths, and I don't do the I'm-not-sure thing because I love this upbeat track, and my mood is lifting, and yes, I really want to dance with him. I can already tell that he's not a self-conscious dancer, that he dances because he likes the music and the rhythm and because it's fun. The sort of person whose confidence increases when they dance.

I don't think about anything else as I sing along to the stupid lyrics, raise my arms and feel my body relax. Brandon takes my hand and twirls and twists me and drops it again and we mirror dance, and I laugh because I can't keep up with him. We dance for ages, and as a slower track comes on, I feel Brandon's arms around my back, and everything else falls away. It's him and me, and I love how he's looking at me, as if he thinks I'm worth gazing at, his eyes deep and soulful. My skin is super-aware of his touch. Craving more contact. I wouldn't even care if Danielle was filming us.

"The best bit of the week has been meeting you," he says. "Of course it sucks that we have to meet here——" He raises his eyes to the dining room, to Morley Hill, and its significance for us. "With you I don't have to pretend that I'm doing OK the whole time."

I nod.

"And you're yourself with me too, right?" he says.

There's an emptiness inside me. I can't speak, so I smile, a deceitful smile, and he leans closer, so close that I feel his hair against my face. When the track finishes, I say, "I'm thirsty. I'll get us some drinks."

"I'll come with you," he says.

"No, I'm fine," I say, and I go before he can argue. At the drinks table, I let people push in in front of me and I spend ages seeing what's there, and pretending to decide which ones to choose. I haven't been honest with Brandon. I've kept him from knowing what I'm really like. Someone who lies rather than admits the terrible part they played in their sister's death. Someone with trust issues. He could do so much better than me. He should set his sights higher.

I take the cans over to the table we were sitting at, now empty. Not even Fay is there. She must have gone back to our room. Brandon sees me and dances over, exaggerating his dance moves.

"I'm not feeling too good," I say as I hand him a lemonade, the same type I saw him drink last night after the quiz. "I'm going to have to go back to the room after I've had this."

More lies. Brandon wants to walk me back to the room, but I shake my head. "Stay. Have fun." I turn away so I can't see his face, but I've already glimpsed the hurt.

The dance floor is crowded. The song is bouncy but there's a couple in a swaying embrace at the edge of the main action. The guy is tall, and he has his large, muscly arms round a much smaller, spindly girl. He's almost pushing her into his chest. It's Joe with Fay.

twenty-two

"There's an explanation," says Fay softly.

My eyes haven't been open more than a few seconds. Fay's sitting up in bed reading her chemistry book, and I've no idea what she's going on about. In the bed between us, Danielle is still lumped under the duvet, breathing heavily. Outside there's the sound of instructors and catering staff arriving for work. Car doors banging. Somebody shouting something about a tangled badminton net.

"Kyra didn't like her birthday being in October because the rest of her family had October birthdays too," says Fay. "So she and Joe decided she should celebrate it in July. It was their tradition. I think it's really sweet."

I wipe the fuzziness from my eyes. It's an explanation

but I don't know that I buy it. "How long did he and Kyra go out for? How much of a tradition was it?"

"I don't know, but Joe said it was a tradition so that's enough for me."

"I wonder why Kyra sent a naked photo of herself to that boy if she was going out with Joe at the time, or was she trying to split up from Joe?"

Fay shakes her head, annoyed. "She got tricked into it."

"How?"

"I don't know, but as Joe says, it's none of your business."

That's me slapped down. I reach for my phone. No messages.

I walk to breakfast on my own. Fay says she felt sick most of the day yesterday because she'd forced herself to eat breakfast so she's not going to make the same mistake today. I don't much want breakfast myself but I want to get out of our room.

Pippa stops me on the steps leading up to the main dining room. "Skye, I was hoping I'd see you. It's a shame you didn't make the talk on resilience yesterday. I've noticed how attached you are to your phone."

I glare at her. There's no way I'm going to let her confiscate it.

"We talked about the pros and cons of social media and online forums."

Does Pippa know about my MessageHound messages?

"We discussed the value of real-life friends versus online strangers," continues Pippa.

Is she trying to warn me? I keep my face as blank as I can.

A crowd of girls are walking across the lawn to the main dining room. We're in the way on these steps. "There are some interesting experiments being done on social media and grief. I'm doing some research in this area myself," says Pippa. She glances at the girls coming towards us. "Anyway, it was a good session. Try and come along to the next one. I think you'll find them useful."

I nod, and move quickly into the dining room before the girls sweep me up with them. My head is whirling as I join the breakfast queue. Is Pippa grooming me to take part in some horrible experiment?

No. I've become completely paranoid.

Nico comes into my head as I pick up a tray from the pile. My whole body loses concentration and the tray clatters to the floor. Why haven't I suspected Nico before now? He'll be coming to the end of his short sentence; he had a good lawyer. I retrieve the tray, grabbing at it a couple of times before gripping it properly. Then there's the man doing time for Luisa's manslaughter. Do prisoners have access to the internet? Have I been tagged wearing my tartan shirt on someone's Instagram or Twitter feed that they might have seen? Could I have been seen by any of the swimming squad? How many people are there who might dislike me this much?

My hand shakes so badly that more cereal ends up on

the tray than in my bowl. I slosh milk over and look round for a table. I want to sit on my own but Kerry is sitting with Joe's room-mates and Rohan whistles to attract my attention to say there's space for me at theirs. At least Joe isn't with them.

"Joe's gone jogging," says Henry. "He woke up in a great mood this morning. Can't think why."

Kerry laughs. "Alice and I had a bet that Skye and Brandon would be the first holiday romance of our group," she says. "And we were nearly right! But it's Fay and Joe. Ahhh." She tilts her head and makes a gushy face, and I don't detect any sarcasm. "Fay not wanting to come to breakfast this morning?"

"Nah, she's reading in bed," I say. I spread out my cereal and pat it, so that it's submerged under the milk, like a lost city.

"They're so sweet together, aren't they?" says Kerry. "She's shy, skinny and clever, and he's big, confident and sporty."

The boys nod. "Joe really likes her," says Rohan.

Am I the only person who doesn't think Fay and Joe make a cute couple?

I don't go straight back to the room after breakfast. I walk to a secluded bench and think about Luisa and Nico, and how nobody could see what was going on until everything went wrong. *Don't forget* the last message said. I open MessageHound and type:

SKYE: I remember everything.

After quitting the app, I check the weather forecast. Overcast but warm. Ten per cent chance of rain.

It was hot and humid the day Luisa died. Mum started the day with a low-grade breakdown. She'd forgotten it was her turn to do the teas and coffees for the support group she was involved in through Oscar. Oscar was going on a play date but she was worried he'd catch a cold from his friend and wouldn't be able to have his operation. In fact she kept taking Oscar's temperature to see if he already had a fever. She tried to get Dad to stay at home to look after him, but Dad had a crucial meeting with his accountant, and he shouted at her that he couldn't believe she'd forgotten and he was already late. On top of that she wasn't ready for a couple of her friends who were coming to stay the night on their way to a holiday cottage, and a fox had done another poo on the trampoline.

I heard all this going on while I lay in bed.

Mum came in and told me to get up, get dressed and make up the bed in the spare room with Luisa before I did anything else, then she went off to tell Luisa the same thing. The slammed front door as she left was a reminder that she meant it.

"You feeling better, Skye?"

Brandon slams me back to reality. He must have had an ultra-quick breakfast or just gone into the dining room to grab the bread roll that's in his hand.

"Er, yeah. Are you all right?"

"Yep." He sits beside me on the bench. If he'd asked whether I minded, I'm not sure what I'd have said.

He stretches out his long legs, and I see his perfect, smooth kneecaps and his long calves. "I hope I didn't say anything stupid last night that ... I don't know ... upset you?"

"No. No. You didn't. I was..."

"Skye," he interrupts. "D'you have a boyfriend back home?"

I feel wrong-footed. "Er, no. No boyfriend. Last night I wasn't feeling very good, but I'm fine this morning."

"OK." He sounds embarrassed now. "I'll see you at the climbing wall, then." He stands up, and I resist the urge to let everything spill out about the messages, about failing to save Luisa. About how I really like him. That would require trust though, and I can't allow myself to make any more mistakes.

"Yes," I say in a voice that sounds horribly like Mum's when she's trying too hard to be bright and cheery. "I'll see you there."

I open MessageHound when Brandon's sufficiently far away.

SKYE: I can't do this any more.

The message shoots back straight away.

LUISA: Why not?

Up ahead, I can still see Brandon walking back to his accommodation block. He's eating the bread roll, and he's definitely not been on his phone. I stare at him, and watch him turn into the path that leads to the door of his building. My message was answered just now. He therefore can't be the person messaging, and whoever's pretending to be Luisa has done me a favour. I can eliminate Brandon as a suspect.

If only I'd trusted him.

A photo appears on my screen because MessageHound is still open. It's of some flowers. White flowers and green foliage on a wooden table. There's no accompanying message. It reminds me of some of the floral tributes at Luisa's funeral. What does it mean? That I deserve to die too?

twenty-three

Today, our last full day before we go home, is the day we jump off a twenty-metre tower at a disused army base. The posters round the main dining hall describe it as a free-fall adrenaline-rush adventure that you don't need a parachute or a bungee cord for, thanks to an invention called a Powerfan which slows the descent. It's what made me excited to go on the activity camp when I first read the leaflet.

But first there's an hour and a half of climbing on the indoor wall at Morley Hill. The instructors tell us to empty our pockets and put the contents in a Tupperware box. I shove a packet of mints in but I hang on to my phone for now.

We take off our shoes and replace them with smelly, battered climbing shoes. After I've stepped into my harness, I watch the others lift each other up by their straps and joke about wedgies. We're issued with helmets, and told to sit on the two benches to wait our turn to climb.

The first two climbers are Henry and Rohan. I watch them climb for a few minutes before I can no longer bear listening to Joe shouting encouragement at them, as if he's their instructor. I turn to my phone and study the photo of the white flowers. I wonder if it means something that I haven't thought of yet, and if I keep racking my brain it will come to me. At first I think my stalker's used a stock photo from the internet but as I enlarge it I think it might be an original shot because the quality isn't great. There's a mark as if there was a tiny smudge on the camera lens when it was taken, and the flowers aren't arranged very neatly. They've gone to some trouble, buying and placing the flowers on a table, and that makes it nastier.

"That was amazing." Brandon takes his helmet off and rubs the top of his head to rebounce his hair. "Did you see me at the top of the wall?" He's slightly sweaty. On a high.

I hesitate, surprised he's already been up and down the wall.

"I don't believe it! You were too busy on your phone to see my moment of glory," says Brandon. He eyes me more closely. "What's up?"

"It's nothing," I say.

"Are you being bullied? You can tell me. Seriously." He steps closer, so no one else can hear. "Joe told me his girlfriend committed suicide because of cyberbullying. That no one realized how bad it was until it was too late. He showed me a photo of the two of them the day before she died. They spent the whole day together and she never said anything about it."

Joe is such an attention junkie.

"Brandon, I'm not being cyberbullied, OK?" *More like stalked.*

"Are you sure? Because if you were, I'd. . ."

Intrigued, I wait for him to finish his sentence, but he trails off, frowning. "What would you do?" I ask.

"I'd do whatever it took to help you."

"Like tell the police? Write a blog post?" He sounds so earnest, I couldn't resist that.

"OK. I don't know what I'd do. But yeah. A blog post. Why not?" He smiles. It dissolves some of the awkwardness that's been there between us this morning.

"I'm touched."

An instructor beckons me over. I stand up and shove my phone into the back pocket of my shorts and fasten the button up to secure it.

"Good luck," says Brandon. "Wave at me from the top. If you get there, that is."

I've done some climbing before, at parties a few years ago, when Annika and the rest of my group were into activities, the more adrenaline-pumping the better. The climbing walls I've been to were easier than this one, though, and not as high. And it was back when I was lighter and fitter.

After I've been attached to the rope, the instructor suggests the first hand- and footholds, and then I'm on my own. It can't be too hard, I tell myself, if the others reached the top. I decide to climb as fast as I can, reaching for each chunk of coloured plastic while scouting ahead for the next one.

There are photos at home of me up trees, on massive climbing frames at adventure playgrounds, at the top of a rope at gym. Once upon a time I was fearless. I didn't think about anything other than getting to the top, or being the quickest. Perhaps I wasn't really that fearless. Perhaps it only felt that way because I had a sister who wasn't into that sort of thing and a little brother who couldn't run or climb or do much because of his heart condition.

"You're doing great!" calls the instructor. "Nearly there."

I visualize touching the ceiling. There's a grimy mark where other people have got there before me on this particular route. For some reason, the image of the flowers drops down at the forefront of my mind, like a top layer over everything else. My arms are burning and my hands are damp with sweat, requiring me to clasp the holds even tighter to stop them slipping. Pain shoots through my stiff, locked fingers. I keep reaching and pulling myself up, super-slowly, like a reptile who hasn't had enough sun.

There's something about the photo that's niggling at me.

"Caught you up," says somebody to my right. Danielle. She is fumbling for the holds but she's going faster than me.

"If you're climbing, you can't be filming me," I say. "That's a bonus."

"The filming's nothing personal," says Danielle. "I like recording the absurd stuff. People always want the sanitized version of an event."

"They don't like being made to look stupid." Three, possibly four more moulded pieces of plastic and I'll be there at the ceiling.

"They want boring." Danielle stops to contemplate the next hold. "They want safe, boring lives."

One ... two ... three ... I'm there. A fraction of a second before Danielle.

I breathe out, and allow myself a glimpse down. Brandon is criss-crossing his arms, waving. I wave back, releasing some tension in my hand, and in my shoulder. His enthusiasm is infectious, and I grin. I even manage a "Woooo!"

"Ready to lower?" shouts the instructor at me.

I nod.

"Lean back into your harness as if you're about to sit down and gently push off the wall with your feet," she calls.

For a split second I feel pure terror as I lean back. The instructor takes my weight on the rope, and the terror is replaced by exhilaration. In the pocket on the back of my shorts I feel my phone shifting and I'm aware that the button must have come off because the phone feels more out than in. I reach for it. Can't grasp it. I'm too late by the tiniest fraction of time.

"Nooo! Watch out!" I scream.

The height of the drop and the weight and speed of the phone equals some terrible velocity. It narrowly misses the instructor's head and cracks down on the floor.

Oh my God.

The instructor swears and the whole place goes silent as I'm lowered to the ground unceremoniously fast. She's shocked. Speechless until her white face turns red. "That was incredibly stupid. You could have seriously injured me."

"I'm so sorry." I feel sick. "Really sorry."

The instructor's eyes are bulging. "Don't you remember me telling you to empty your pockets?"

I lower my eyes. *Stupid, stupid, stupid.*

"Pick your phone up and sit out the rest of this session on the bench."

Brandon has already picked up my phone. "The screen's cracked," he says as he hands it to me.

I plonk myself down on the bench. Shaking. "I could have given her a head injury," I say.

Brandon shrugs. "But you didn't. Sometimes the worst

doesn't happen." He gestures towards my phone. "Is it working?"

I switch it on and peer at the cracked screen. Nothing's happening. *Crap*. It's totalled. I feel cut off already.

"You can use mine," says Brandon. "It's back in my room, but I'll get it later."

"Thanks." I guess I should text Mum as soon as I can to say I've damaged my phone. It might pre-empt her from harassing Pippa or the local police force when I fail to clock in.

Not having access to MessageHound might be a relief. Given his odd behaviour over Kyra's birthday and at the paintballing, Joe is the most likely person to be sending the messages. If it is him, then he knows my phone is out of action, and the madness might stop.

I think about the flower photo, and the troubling thought that there's a meaning or a visual clue which I've missed. Have I seen those flowers in a vase somewhere at Morley Hill?

"I've had enough of climbing," says Brandon. He drops down on to the same bench as me, and removes his climbing shoes and a pair of black trainer socks, and I like that he's so close to me that our shoulders are almost touching. As he sits there, wriggling his toes, picking out a piece of fluff that's caught between two of them, I realize this is an act of solidarity. He specializes in them.

We watch the others do their second climbs. "I've lost loads of unbacked-up photos of my sister," I say, my voice flat with this sudden awful knowledge. I hold my hands up. "Don't tell me I should have copied them. I meant to."

"There's a little shop, near where I live, that's got a rep for repairing phones and getting data off them," Brandon says. "It's like a junk shop with loads of spare parts for things everywhere. I could take your phone in there, if you like. See what they say."

I know there's not much hope, but it's something. "Thanks. I'll give it to you tomorrow before we leave." I clutch it in my hands. He has no idea how hard it will be for me to hand it over to him, even though I know he can't access any information on it.

"My mate dropped his phone from the top of a roller coaster – they couldn't help him. But the roller coaster was much higher than that wall and there wasn't a mat at the bottom."

"My dad's phone went through the washing machine," I say. "That didn't recover either."

We trade phone-disaster stories. Brandon tells me about a friend of his mum's who left her phone on top of her car for some unknown reason. She drove off and the car behind ran it over. It's a terrible story but I can't help laughing. For a few moments, before I remember my own phone again, the weirdness of MessageHound, and last summer, I feel almost happy.

"I don't know why you were laughing after what you did," says Joe when the session is over and he walks past us. "You think there's one rule for you and another for everyone else, don't you? You've got a lot to learn."

I can't find enough breath to speak for a moment. Joe frightens me with his arrogant and untrustworthy eyes. "It was. . . I didn't. . ." I stumble over the words.

"Leave it," says Brandon. "He's not worth it."

twenty-four

The tower is a short minibus ride away. The whole of Yellow Group comes, even if they're not keen on doing the jump, because of the photo and video opportunities at the top. We see the grey metal cylinder of the tower long before we turn into the abandoned army training ground. It's old and industrial, and scary.

We step down from the minibus and stare up at it.

"It's like something in a nightmare," says Fay.

"It looks like the film set for a dystopian thriller," says Brandon. "The final fight scene would obviously be at the top of the tower."

Pippa gathers us round her. "As someone who's done this jump several times, I'm here to tell you that it's a phenomenal experience. There's a fast descent from the top, and then a gentle landing." She holds her hand up and pushes at the air as she says, "*But* there is no pressure on anyone to jump. You can get kitted up, take the lift to the top and change your mind. Enjoy the view and come back down with me in the lift."

I cram into the lift with the first half of the group, after making sure I'm in a different half to Joe. I don't want to have to hear him dish out jumping advice, or be accidentally wedged up against him. All chat stops as the doors close.

"It's OK," says the jump instructor who's with us, "nobody's died doing this. Yet." I guess no one's told him that that we're on a bereaved kids' holiday.

We step out of the lift on to a metal mesh floor, creaky and insubstantial. There's more of a breeze up here and I swear the air is thinner – I need to take deeper breaths.

When everybody's at the top, we're offered the choice of organizing ourselves into the order in which we'd like to jump, or picking numbers from a hat. Henry is desperate to go first; the rest of us shuffle into an approximation of a queue. I'm eighth, behind Brandon and in front of Danielle. Joe stands back, saying he'll take whichever position is left. Fay hovers near him. She becomes eleventh, and Joe is twelfth.

"You can opt out at any point, right up until you step off the platform," says the main instructor. "Nobody gets pushed."

There's nervous laughter. Some people are wavering. I understand it, but I'm not one of them. My stomach is doing figures of eight and my windpipe has narrowed, but I'm going to jump. I want to know what it feels like to free-fall. To feel brave.

There are metal benches to sit on. Everything here is metal and ugly. There's the safety talk. The please-behave-responsibly-once-you're-on-the-ground talk. And then Henry and Rohan are taken away, down the short ladder on to the platform. We crowd round the railings and see Henry have his harness fastened to a rope. He turns to give us a thumbs up and then he steps into the air, and screams.

Brandon turns away, and goes to sit on a bench. I follow him.

"I feel sick," he says.

"Nerves," I say.

He takes a deep breath and sighs it out. "What if I throw up?"

"Depends which way the wind's blowing. Could be messy."

Pippa is pointing out local landmarks to Danielle, who's filming, though probably not the sights that Pippa thinks she is. I hear something about an ancient burial ground. A geological explanation for the tallest hill. And rumbling below Pippa's voice is Joe's. He's with Fay, further round the tower than Pippa, but they're not admiring the view.

185

"Everything begins with a single step," he says. Fay nods as Joe drivels on with his motivational speech. The next thing I can make out is, "This is a test, Fay. D'you understand?"

"What's he going on about?" I ask Brandon.

"Who?" Brandon has no idea what I'm talking about. He follows my gaze. "Joe? I didn't hear what he said."

"Something about the jump being a test."

"A test of courage?" Brandon places his hand on his chest. "I get that. My heart's racing already."

Fay has turned away from Joe, and I see that she's on the brink of tears. Her legs are shaking and she's curled over, as if she's expecting to be hit. Like a skin-and-bone dog on an advert for the RSPCA.

"He's putting pressure on her," I say to Brandon.

"You think so?" says Brandon. "Don't worry. Pippa's here. She'll make sure Fay doesn't jump unless she wants to." He looks towards the platform. "Shit. Person number six is about to jump... That means I'm next."

Joe is still speaking to Fay, his voice too low to hear. Fay wipes an eye with the back of her hand. The metal flooring makes so much noise, they look round at me as I walk towards them.

"Fay, if you don't want to jump, don't."

Joe adjusts the waistband of his shorts, flashing a section of his six-pack or eight-pack or whatever he's got going on there. "Er, this has got nothing to do with you, Skye."

"Fay's upset, so yes it has." I look into her tear-swollen eyes. "You don't want to do this jump, do you?"

For a moment it seems she hasn't understood what I've said. Like something catastrophic has happened to her IQ. And then she shakes her head.

"See," I say. I regret the triumph in my voice as soon as I've said it, but I knew I was right.

Joe shrugs; his face shows no emotion. "It's completely Fay's decision," he says. He puts his arm round her shoulder, draws her to him. She snuggles against him, as if she's getting herself warm. I stare at her, amazed that one person can be both so clever and so stupid.

"Skye!" calls Brandon. He's standing by the ladder to the platform. "We're next. Come on."

As we step on to the metal decking of the platform, one of the instructors says, "It's like being on the top of a diving board, isn't it?" He doesn't wait for an answer. Claps his hands, and asks, "OK, folks, so who's first?"

Brandon holds his hand up. "Me. But if Skye wants to go first, I'm OK with that." He has his back to the ledge, a couple of metres away from us, where you step forward into nothingness.

"I don't care. I just want to get on with it," I say. A discussion is the last thing I need right now.

"I'll go next," says Brandon. "Before I change my mind." I like that he doesn't try to fake the fear in his voice. He steps on to the ledge. "Here goes."

Once he's ready to jump, Brandon looks at me.

Everything is in that look. Strength and weakness. The whole of him. And he disappears with more of a shout than a scream, and I yell, "Whoooooooo!" All at once, my voice feels as if it's the strongest part of my body.

"Is he down? Is he all right?" I ask the instructor, who's leaning over the ledge to check the rope.

"Yeah, peachy," he says. He calls across to his colleague, "What number are we on now, dude?"

"I'm number eight," I say, in case his colleague has lost count. "Skye Colton." Perhaps he'll take more care of me if he knows me by name rather than by number.

After the instructor tells me I'm good to go, I stand on the ledge.

You can do this.

I step. The breath is snatched from my mouth and then I scream. I experience the pure rush of being alive. The blur of colour.

As I free-fall, I have a moment of clarity. I need to go back to Yew Tree House. If there's an opportunity to be free from the crippling hold it has over me, I have to take it.

twenty-five

Brandon is right in front of me. De-helmeted. De-harnessed. "Isn't it the coolest thing?" He grabs me for a hug, and he laughs as he untangles his shirt from my harness when we pull apart. "Didn't you feel ridiculously brave?" He's so happy. Eyes shining. Talking. Talking.

We sit on a patch of grass with the others. In a circle. Sharing stories, watching the next person jump. Cheering. I remove my helmet, harness, trainers and my socks. The grass is soft and mossy. It feels pleasant against my toes with their silly copycat nails.

I'll go to Pitford this afternoon. The schedule is flexible. Swimming. Some workshop or other. Rounders, perhaps. It'll be my last chance before I leave Morley Hill tomorrow.

The next person jumps, their body minuscule against the tower. When they reach the bottom safely, I lie back on the grass and place my hand on my stomach. My breathing is deep, even, almost perfect. Everyone's voices are reduced to a murmur. After a bit, I'm aware of a shadow over my face, and move my head to see who it is. Brandon places a hand on my leg, his dark skin against mine like a statement. "You're quiet."

I smile up at him, my leg hot beneath his touch. "Thinking."

"What are you thinking?"

"That I want to go and see my old house this afternoon."

"Want me to come with you?" He's distracted by something someone shouts at him and he calls back, "Wait a moment."

"Don't worry," I say when I have his attention again. "It'll be boring for you."

"All right. I'll practise bombing into the pool instead. They don't let you do that in many places. Need to make the most of it."

I sit up and brush stray grass from the backs of my legs. Feel the criss-cross patterns the indentations have made. If he'd sounded more like he wanted to come, I'd have said yes.

Everyone's eyes are on the tower. Watching the latest jumpee. Brandon's face in profile is beautiful. He'd score highly if he was measured for symmetry. When the holiday ends, we might keep in touch online for a bit, but I doubt I'll sit next to him again like this.

He turns to me. "Fay made it down, then."

I look towards the tower. At the figure touching down on the ground. Yes, it's Fay.

"Joe must have persuaded her," I say.

The group is hollering at her. Calling her over to our little group on the grass. She comes slowly. Dazed, as if she can't believe what she's just done.

"I was so scared," she says, kneeling at the edge of the group, her voice shaky. "I did it though. I did it, didn't I?"

"You certainly did," says Brandon. "Get the official photo from the website later. As proof."

"What made you do it?" I ask. I follow Fay's gaze and glance up at the ledge at the top of the tower. The figure up there is Joe. I bet he wants us all to admire him.

"I did it for him," she says.

On the minibus back to the centre, Fay sits with Joe, her eyes closed and her head against his arm like a sleeping child against an adult. Joe received a massive cheer when he jumped, and again when he touched down. All of us were on our feet by then. All twelve of us had made it, but it was more than that. Joe finished it in style, waving at us, like some singer descending on stage at a concert. Pippa came down in the lift with people's cameras and other possessions and made a point of thanking him for helping Fay get over her nerves. He brushed it off, mumbled something about being proud of her, then caught my eye. Held it and nodded ever so slightly.

"Joe makes me uncomfortable," I say to Brandon, turning back round after a quick stare at him and Fay.

"He thinks he knows it all," says Brandon. I wonder if he's aware that one of his legs is millimetres away from mine. "Perhaps he's, like, compensating because of his girlfriend committing suicide. Making himself into something important, you know, to feel better about himself?"

"Maybe," I say, but I think Brandon is simply a nicer person than me and is making excuses for him.

"Bereavement does weird things to people," he says. "Look at my dad. He used to be this easy-going family man, and then after my brother died he did a runner to the States and became a workaholic. Both times I went to visit him, he didn't bother to take a single day off work. I know he has to work hard, but I'm his only kid now. You know what I'm saying?"

I nod. I think of Mum and Dad, who blame themselves for not noticing what Luisa was up to because they were so busy watching over their child with the heart condition and worrying about Dad's business. Now they want to set up some campaign to educate people about drugs, like there aren't enough already. As if they're scared we won't remember Luisa in a positive way unless they do that. Maybe the person to tell them it's not necessary is going to have to be me.

"My dad keeps saying he's going to come over here for a holiday but it's never happened. He sends me designer shirts and thinks *Job done*."

"I've noticed your shirts. . ." I say.

He holds out the bottom of the checked shirt he's wearing and frowns. It has a hedgehog symbol embroidered on the sleeve and collar. "They're bad, aren't they? But I figured it wouldn't matter if they got ripped or ruined during the activities. I should have brought a few of my real T-shirts. They are *awesome*."

I raise an eyebrow.

"Awesome because I've chosen them. They're waaay scruffier."

The minibus turns in to Morley Hill's drive and parks outside the reception building. As we wait for Pippa to open the sliding door from the outside, I ask around for nail varnish remover. No one has any but Alice says she has some blue nail varnish in her washbag that I can borrow.

The nail varnish is the blue of a well-maintained swimming pool. Bright and flawless.

Wedging my foot securely against the wooden frame of the bed, I apply it to my toenails, over the top of the red and pink. Ten minutes behind Fay, Danielle goes off to the pool, banging the door behind her.

All I can hear are the distant shouts of people outside. I lie back on my bed to let the nail varnish dry.

The loud knocking at the door is a shock. "Who is it?" I shout.

"Brandon. I've got my phone. I thought you might want to text your mum."

I appraise my toes. They're still glistening. Not yet dry. "Hang on." I hobble to the door on my heels so the toenails don't touch each other, and open the door. "Excuse the smell of nail varnish."

Brandon hands me the phone and walks in. He hovers until I point him towards Danielle's bed. Being a boy, he's not supposed to be in D block, let alone my room, but I don't let that worry me if it doesn't worry him.

I sit on my bed, check my toes, then begin to type my text message to Mum. I keep it short.

"Thanks." I prepare to shuffle over to Danielle's bed and hand him back the phone. "Hope she doesn't text you back a load of nonsense."

"No problem." He stands up to collect his phone. "I was thinking. Everyone's going to be pissed off if I practise my bombing in the pool. I'll come to Pitford with you. If you're OK with that?" He nods towards my toes. "When the nail varnish is dry."

My heart spins. "Yes. Sure," I say.

twenty-six

We go the back way, over the gate. At the narrow lane, we turn left, towards the village. It doesn't take long to work out that the only bus stop is on the main road.

When the bus arrives, it's already packed with old people, and we have to stand and be stared at. At Hoathley, we wait for the next bus outside the United Reformed Church, which has a low wall outside it. I sat here with Luisa countless times, before she passed her driving test. Today I stay hunched next to Brandon, my eyes on the pavement, hoping that no one will recognize me.

On the bus to Pitford I tell Brandon about the messages. I speak hesitantly; it's been so long since I properly confided in someone.

"Anyone who pretends to be a dead person online has got to be a psycho," says Brandon. His shocked expression comforts me because he recognizes how horrible this has been. "Why didn't you tell me earlier?"

I could lie, but there doesn't seem any point. "You were one of my suspects. But I know it couldn't have been you because of the timing of one of the messages."

"Okaaay," says Brandon. He looks upset.

I say gently, "I didn't want it to be you, but I couldn't trust *anybody*."

He nods slowly, as if he's still thinking about it, and says, "I'm glad I've been eliminated. You should tell Pippa about this when we get back though."

"Maybe," I say. "But I'd rather handle this myself." As soon as an adult gets involved, it'll be blown up into an even worse thing, and Mum and Dad will probably ban me from any form of messaging for ever.

Brandon places his arm along the top of the bus seat, almost round my shoulder, and asks me who I think might be responsible.

"Anyone at Morley Hill, basically," I say. "It's possible someone from my old life might have recognized me when I was wearing my tartan shirt in the village, but I think it's Joe. I just need proof."

He nods. "Yeah, my money would be on him too."

"I hate how he's got Fay sucked into his little world," I say. Discussing this out loud, trusting Brandon enough to reveal some of the thoughts in my head, gives me a sense of calm. Being away from the claustrophobic atmosphere of Morley Hill helps too. I close my eyes and prepare myself to see my old home, the only one I'd known until nine months ago. I picture each part of the house, starting with Luisa's bedroom, so I can practise keeping my panic under control. I sweep through each room and into the garden, where I force myself to remember the pool that I once loved so much.

The big DIY store where we have to get off appears sooner than I'm ready for it. We step down from the bus, into familiar territory that feels foreign. Like I've returned after a war.

We cross at the lights, and turn into the road signed to Pitford. We pass the discount pine furniture warehouse where Luisa's friend used to work on Saturdays, the Crown pub, and houses set back from the road with high glossy hedges to block out the main road. In between the whoosh of cars going by, we hear the shouts of kids playing in gardens and the whine of electrical garden equipment. If we kept going, through the centre of the village, towards the play-park, we'd come to Annika's road.

I'm happier after we've turned right and right again, and there's less chance of running into her or anyone from my old school. Here the houses are much further apart, and some have horseboxes in the drive. There's still a low table outside the bungalow where the road bends. For sale: runner beans, radishes with earth on them, bumpy cucumbers, and punnets of raspberries. One jar of berry jam. There's a wooden honesty box. Brandon swipes a radish, wipes it on his shorts and crunches it. I smile at his contorted face when the bitterness kicks in. He shudders theatrically. I envy him his clear conscience. Did he feel the same piercing anxiety when he returned to his old house where he'd lived with his brother as I do now? The fear that he would unravel?

The signs are visible now. The first one says *FARM SHOP. FREE PARKING.* There's an arrow. The second sign says *LOWER ROAD FARM AND YEW TREE HOUSE.* My insides tighten.

There's never been a proper road here. Just a track with potholes and big lumps of grey-white stone. Smaller stones too, some of them sharp. Luisa and I would challenge ourselves when we were younger to walk barefoot down the track to see who could bear the pain best.

The steep, grassy banks have their July colour – white, yellow, and a few pink flowers, and the drone of insects is loud in the hush of the afternoon. The dark-stained wooden fence marking the boundary of Yew Tree House begins near the bottom of the track, but the house itself isn't visible through the leafy trees until a little further up. Brandon asks if there are any yew trees in the garden and I tell him there's one big one at the end of the garden that is supposed to be hundreds of years old. I don't know if he's distracting me on purpose, but it helps.

"Yew Tree House is huge," he says, when the top part of the back of the house is visible.

"It was the old farmhouse," I say. "The new farmhouse is a bungalow at the top of the track, behind the farm shop."

"Your family has money, then?" asks Brandon.

"We used to. My dad made a load, and then his business crashed," I say. The word *crash* is misleading. I make it sound as if it happened suddenly, rather than something which hovered over us for a long time.

We carry on past the bit of Yew Tree House garden where you can glimpse the low roof of the pool building that has the changing room, shower, toilet and heating equipment in it, but I don't point it out to Brandon. I keep walking.

No one's in the pool or we'd be able to hear them. Brandon's wearing a hoody, but it's definitely outdoor swimming weather. Dad told me the house had been sold to a family with young children. Max Tomkins told me that the family must be from out of the area or they'd never have bought the house if they'd known that a teenager had died there. Either that or they'd bought it for way less than it was worth.

We stayed in the house while Oscar recovered from his operation, then we moved in October half-term. Lots of our furniture had to be sold or go into storage because it wouldn't fit in the rented flat.

The big metal gate is shut across the driveway. I've

never seen it closed before. When we're nearer I read the new rectangular sign on it.

Yew Tree House
Private property
Press buzzer for entry

I lean against the gate, and feel an intense longing to be back in this house, pre-Nico. It's inconceivable that Luisa no longer exists. That she's not gone out in Mum's car, or isn't lying on a sofa in the long living room on her mobile, a nearly finished packet of salt and vinegar crisps on the low table next to her. That I'll never see her again.

My stomach liquefies and there's the horrifying possibility that I'm going to be sick, here by the gate post.

Brandon grasps my arm lightly. "Are you OK?" He steers me across the track to the grassy verge. "Why don't you sit for a moment?"

We sit with our legs sticking out on to the track, pale dust from the stones rising in the growing heat and clinging to them. Familiar farm noises. The faint scent of the wild flowers. Brandon talks, his words a reassuring rumble. I fix my eyes on my old house. It's been done up a little. Paint. New plants. Same but different. Indifferent. I feel lost, anchorless. Further from Luisa than ever.

"I'm guessing you don't want me to buzz the buzzer and ask if you can go in?" says Brandon.

My are-you-mad face gives him my answer. The family would be horrified by my grim pilgrimage. "I'm ready to head back," I tell Brandon. I need to go before my composure slips. Before I'm spotted by anyone from my previous life.

"Would you mind if I went to the farm shop?" asks Brandon as we stand up. "Got something to eat?" He sees my reluctance. "I'll be really quick and you can stay here."

"No, I'll come with you," I say.

If Toby's there, it'll be awkward, but part of me wants to see the farm shop one last time. As part of this goodbye process. Toby and I spoke at Luisa's funeral, the bit afterwards that was in a hotel in Hoathley, but already it was stiff and formal, as if we hardly knew each other. He called round a few times after Luisa died, but all he did was go on about how he couldn't believe she was gone, so I stopped answering the doorbell, and let Mum do the polite-chat thing at the door.

During our last few weeks here my stomach hurt every time I glanced out of my bedroom window and saw the pool, sometimes so badly I'd double over with the pain. Dad owed so much money that we hardly bought anything from the farm shop any more, and Oscar was scared to be in the house unless all the doors and windows were locked.

"They do cakes here, right?" asks Brandon, and I nod.

There are three cars, including the battered old farm-shop Volvo, parked in front of the shop. Customers. Anyone for the farm itself would have gone through the gateway to the left and parked in the farmyard. The silver metal buckets of flowers outside the shop are new. So is the black sandwich board with special offers written on it in chalk, but everything else is achingly familiar. An oldish woman and someone who might be her daughter come out of the shop, and the daughter holds the door for us. Brandon runs ahead to take it from her, and I've stepped through the door before I'm fully prepared.

I scan the shop to see who's working today, hoping for Wendy or Carol from the village, but almost immediately I see Toby. Stacking a chiller cabinet with clear plastic tubs of olives. He thinks the clanking of the bell attached to the door is because of the customers leaving, not us arriving. I'm aware of a tall man with a grey beard selecting fruit super carefully, but he's on the edge of my vision, and I can't take my eyes off Toby. He still has the same chunky build, but his shoulders are more drooped and his face is stubbly, though it's not edgy stubble. His thick brown hair is flatter and thinner. He's lost his energy. I can't imagine him challenging anyone to a race to the cowshed any more.

"I'll check out the cakes," says Brandon, and Toby looks up. Shock flashes across his face.

"Skye? What are you doing here?"

I'm not ready to speak yet. My brain is recalibrating, trying to work out how to cope with being here again. Before last summer, Toby would be flicking an olive at me by now. Today he stares at me as if I've returned from the dead.

202

"I'm staying at Morley Hill," I say eventually. "The other side of Hoathley. An activity camp. I thought I'd come over to Pitford, seeing as it wasn't that far away." It's Mum's over-cheery voice again.

"Right."

Hugging doesn't seem appropriate. I've been in the same bed as him, had snowball fights, been close, but we've never hugged.

"They use your chilli sauce there."

"Yeah?" he says, and moves away from the chiller cabinet. The man with the grey beard wants to pay for his fruit. I join Brandon by the cakes and hold a cardboard cake box open for him as he picks up an enormous slice of lemon drizzle cake with the tongs. I shake my head when he goes to pick up a second slice for me.

"This is Brandon, by the way," I say when it's our turn to be served.

Toby nods and takes Brandon's money, his attention still on the man striding out of the shop, who calls "Cheerio" at the door.

"You finally thought you'd get in touch?" says Toby, pushing the till drawer shut and handing back change.

This isn't how I wanted the conversation to go. "I—"

"You didn't come and say goodbye when you moved. I didn't even know you'd gone until Mum told me." Toby walks towards the stable-type door that leads out to the farmyard. As if he needs fresh air. The top half of it is open, and I can see the barn where the tractors are housed.

"It happened quickly," I say. A blush spreads up from my neck.

"I noticed you defriended me."

You were too needy.

"It's OK," he says. "You don't have to explain." He switches his gaze to Brandon. "She's told you what happened at her house last summer?"

It hadn't occurred to me that Toby might want to talk about what happened.

"Yes," says Brandon. "I know about her sister."

"It's still a big story round here," says Toby. "Drugs and manslaughter."

Brandon's momentarily startled.

Don't say any more. I lean against the counter to take some weight off my wobbly legs. It's smooth and solid, made from an old tree that came down in a storm when Toby's dad was a boy.

"Luisa and I went out together for a couple of years," says Toby to Brandon. "We were really close. She got in with a bad crowd at uni. She was the last person you'd think would be involved with drugs." The aggressive tone to Toby's voice is new. He used to be a much softer person.

Brandon secures the lid of his cake box. "It happens," he says, and I'm grateful that he's so matter-of-fact. I like that he's here and not bombing into the pool at Morley Hill.

"So how are you doing, Toby?" I ask, to change the subject. To make him happier.

He neatens a row of granola packets. "Busy. Doing more deliveries."

I'm about to tell him I wasn't talking about the shop, but he says, "What about you? What d'you think of Morley Hill?"

What d'you think of Moorly Hill? Toby hated writing and spelling. My skin prickles with alarm.

I want you to be happy but I'm upset with you.

Don't forget.

"Someone's been sending me messages, pretending to be Luisa," I say. "D'you know anything about them?"

I'm aware Brandon's staring at me.

Toby screws his face up. "No. What messages? Is that the real reason why you're here? Not because you want to see me. You want to accuse me of sending messages."

"I just. . ." Am I going mad? Why would Toby want to stalk me? How could he have seen me in my tartan shirt? Could it have been him in the white van when we were in the village? Does the farm shop do deliveries in a van these days? I go to the shop window. I don't remember there being one out there but perhaps I just didn't notice. Nope. But the buckets of flowers catch my eye. There are different bunches, colour-themed. I see a couple with white flowers and greenery.

"The white flowers. . ." I say.

"They're eight ninety-nine," says Toby. "Two for fifteen. Want some?"

"No." I need to clear my head.

"They were Luisa's favourite," says Toby. "Roses and freesias."

They were? I picture Toby lifting a bunch out of the bucket for Luisa and handing it to her, the water dripping from the stems. Then I know. Running back to the counter, I place my hands on the smooth wooden surface, on the tiny bleached area that I thought was a smudge on the camera lens.

Toby's my stalker. He placed those flowers on here.

"Do you want me to recreate that horrible photo of the flowers here?" I say. "We can check it against the original." My phone is lying broken in Morley Hill, but if I absolutely had to, I might be able to download MessageHound on Brandon's.

Toby's eyes flit to Brandon and back to me. "I thought you'd like the flowers."

"You bastard," says Brandon. "Of course she didn't like the flowers."

"You terrified me," I say.

Toby winces. "I didn't want to terrify you. I wanted to shake you up a bit. Make you think about things."

Rage rips through me. "You think I need shaking up?" I recall the silly hope I'd had that it was actually Luisa contacting me, the confusion and fear. Not being able to trust Brandon. "How could you?"

I run.

Toby shouts, "Wait, Skye. Please. I want to explain," but I keep running. Out of the shop, to the far end of the car park, to the gate Luisa, Toby and I used to like sitting on as kids, rattling it so we'd have to hang on as tightly as we could. I fling myself against it and bury my head in my arms, breathing in the metal smell of the gate as tears drench my hot skin. Toby was someone I would have trusted with my life.

How can the Toby who sat on this gate, and lay about in snow, on grass, and in Luisa's bed with me, who let me help in the shop way before I was any use, change into a person who would hurt me so deeply? So willingly. I think of all those times I pretended I was a Mulligan, not a Colton. Of my secret fantasy that Luisa would marry Toby and we'd all live happily ever after.

How did it all go wrong?

Two sets of footsteps make their way over the rough stones in the car park. One set arrives before the other, and I feel a hand on my back. I know it's Brandon before he says, "You should talk about this with Toby."

"Skye, I'm sorry. I was a jerk." Toby sounds like he did when was younger, apologizing for a game involving cowpats that had gone too far. My fury loosens a notch.

"Why did you do it?" I say, wheeling round as I wipe my nose on my arm because it's that or the bottom of my T-shirt. "That account was private."

"I didn't set out to do it," he says, looking down at a big stone that he's pushing with the toe of his work boot. "I do things which make me feel close to Luisa. I want to let go, but I can't. It's too soon. So I hang out with her old friends, eat salt and vinegar crisps in Hoathley cinema, look at photos. After we split up she didn't MessageHound me any more. Said it was too much faff. But I knew you two still used it sometimes and you stored photos. I wanted to see the photos, ones I hadn't seen before."

"Didn't Luisa change her passcode after you split up?"

He lifts his head. "She changed it from her birthday to yours. I'd seen her do it loads of times when I was delivering to your house. She never changed her username."

I shake my head. Using birthdays as a passcode. How predictable. But it was *my* birthday she used. Fresh tears sting my eyes.

"You sent that message saying how much you missed Luisa," says Toby. "I missed her too. I couldn't help replying, and then . . . I got carried away. I was upset." He sees me wipe my eyes with the back of my hand. "Come on. I've got some kitchen roll in the shop."

I look at Brandon, who nods.

Perhaps it's because we're not making eye contact, but Toby speaks more easily as we walk back to the shop. He explains that he saw me at Morley Hill on Monday when he was doing an afternoon delivery there, and again in the village. He'd borrowed the van for a catering event. "Each time I wanted to say hello," he says, "but I didn't because I thought you might blank me."

"I wouldn't have done," I say, but I know I would have

been embarrassed. I'd have tried to get away as soon as possible.

We're in the shop. Brandon perches on the stool that's used for reaching high shelves. Toby leans behind the counter for the kitchen paper and breaks off a couple of sheets for me. "I couldn't be sure," he says. "You didn't want to have anything to do with me for the last few months." He takes a deep breath. "I was envious that you were having a nice time at the camp. I wanted my voice heard for a change. Except –" he pulls a face "– I know it wasn't my voice; it was Luisa's."

I see it. How we dropped him. First Luisa, then the rest of the family. Our families had been entwined all our lives and I didn't take any of that into account. I never thought about how much Toby loved Luisa, even though she didn't have time for him any more. He loved the rest of us too. I blow my nose, and chuck the paper in the bin behind the counter.

"I know it's been hell for your family," he says. "But my family have had a rough time too. We miss her."

"Even though she changed?"

He nods. "To be honest, I think she was just going through a phase. Like when she became a vegan."

And it's back. His sweetness. Us being us. I don't want to scream at him any more. I see in his face how he's only just been coping.

"I really am sorry," he says. He rubs one eye and he looks so tired I wonder if he has trouble sleeping too.

"I'm sorry too," I say.

"You know what, I've missed your help in the shop."

"Is that because no one else will accept the pitiful amount you paid me?" I half smile.

"Partly."

The hostility between us has disappeared, but it's still stilted. "How are the customers?" I ask.

"They're fine," he says. "No more of a pain in the arse than usual."

The barking in the farmyard makes me jump. "Kip!" I say.

"Want to see him?" asks Toby, though it's a question he doesn't need to ask.

I glance at Brandon, who's opening his cake box, and follow Toby to the stable door. When Toby unbolts the bottom half and whistles, Kip comes bounding towards us, ears flying. I squat to greet him and he charges into me, waggling his whole body and panting bad breath.

"He recognizes you," says Toby. Out of all the farm dogs, Kip was always the one most likely to appreciate anyone showing an interest in him.

"Who's moved into Yew Tree House?" I say when Kip has quit throwing himself at me, and is sitting with his tongue panting, ears pricked.

"A family with six-year-old twins," says Toby. "They're away on holiday at the moment. We're keeping an eye on the place for them."

"So it wouldn't matter if Skye wanted to have a look

round before we go back to Morley Hill?" says Brandon.

I bite my lip. Do I want to do that?

"One of you could climb over the fence into the garden, I guess," says Toby. "Unbolt the gate in the wall at the bottom, unless they've padlocked it. There's CCTV at the front of the house, the side gate and above the patio doors."

Brandon lobs his empty cake box into the bin behind the counter. "What d'you think, Skye?"

I see the red water, and Luisa's seaweed hair. But I was brave enough to leap from the tower. Brave enough to come this far. "OK, I'll do it."

twenty-seven

Scaling the wooden fence isn't going to be easy. It's high, there's nothing to hold on to and there are no weak points. It's not that sort of garden. On the plus side, the new people haven't added glass or barbed wire along the top, or a note saying that it's covered with anti-climbing paint.

"I'll give you a leg up," Brandon says. "What's the other side of here?"

"A flower bed."

"So a good place to climb over?"

"As good as any other," I say. I squish his arm muscles. "Are you ready?"

"Bring it on," says Brandon. He stands sideways against the fence with his hands clasped, palms upwards, for me to step on. "Try and push off against my hands while I lift you."

We listen for cars; then I do a little run-up and shove my canvas shoe in the stirrup he's made with his hands. We're not quite in time, I wobble, and although I can reach the top of the fence, I'm too low to pull myself up.

"Ow."

"Practice run," says Brandon, after I've slid back to the ground and checked out the graze on my leg where it scraped against the fence. "After three." He begins the count straight away, and on three I place my foot more firmly in his hands and push down hard as he propels me upwards. I grasp the top of the fence and my arms shake as I force them to take my weight, levering myself up. The moment I glimpse over the top into the garden, I wobble but I keep my balance and haul myself to the point at which I know I can clear the fence in a clumsy vault.

I land in a clump of pale pink flowers. "I'm fine, in case you were wondering," I call to Brandon as I attempt to resurrect the flowers by fluffing them up.

Very little has changed in the garden. It's ordered and pretty, with pink, purple and white flowers in between the various greens. Still no yellow or orange blooms, colours which weren't part of Mum's scheme. The lawn is stripy, neatly edged. There's a different style of wooden garden furniture on the patio. I take in the CCTV camera on the back of the house that points down at the patio doors, and the new alarm box.

And then I force myself to confront the pool area. The glass fencing is still there. Beyond it the pool, with its cover rolled back tightly, gleams. Blue, not red.

"I'll go down to the wall," calls Brandon. "See you at the gate."

"OK. Give me a moment," I shout back, except my voice cracks and sounds so thin he might not have heard me.

Be brave.

I walk across the soft lawn to tackle the childproof gate. The simultaneous squeezing and lifting routine works first time, like it did that day last summer. It's weird the tiniest of details that stay in your head, etched deeply for no reason.

There's a new bench, pushed up against the changing room building. Turquoise plastic. It looks great. Better than our wicker chairs, which had to go inside at the first drop of rain, and snagged the fabric of swimming costumes if you didn't use one of the white seat cushions.

It's hard to look at the changing room. I tug at the door, hoping it's locked. It is. There's the plant with the small white flowers that I could smell at Morley Hill. I touch the enormous plant pot that it's growing out of and the sweet, overpowering fragrance wafts over me.

My shoes are disproportionately noisy on the hard pale stone as I walk towards the place where Luisa smashed her head. There's no damage to the stone, no lingering bloodstain. Who scrubbed it clean? Crouching down on to one knee, I dip my hand in the pool, and recoil straight away. If my counsellor were here, she'd say, *Why did you do that, Skye?*

There's no reason. This is clean water. Nothing bad can happen. I lean forward and try again, cupping the water in one hand and holding it until it leaks away. The smell of chlorine reaches my nostrils and I almost gag.

According to family legend, I could swim before I could walk. It was my thing – the skill that differentiated me from Luisa and Oscar. This pool always felt as if it belonged to me. The tiles, darker blue than in most pools, the sudden drop to the deep end, and the way when you swam in the direction of the house, you could see through the glass panels across the garden.

"Skye?" Brandon's shout sounds worried.

I leave the pool area and run to the tall brick wall at the bottom of the garden, into the shade of the trees where clouds of insects vibrate, and the grass is springy in between tree roots. The new family have revamped the compost heap with a new wooden structure. The intense smell of grass cuttings hits the back of my nose.

There's a wheelbarrow in front of the gate, which I move. The bolts are as rusty as ever. No padlocks.

"Skye?"

"I'm here," I say through the gate. I prepare to slide the reluctant bolts back, wary of my hands slipping or my skin being caught.

One bolt has to be coaxed across by wiggling it; the

other slams back. Brandon helps inch the gate open enough to squeeze himself through from the field.

"Welcome to my old garden," I say.

"Nice," he says, walking ahead to the main lawn. He stops when he sees the pool, and I catch him up.

"Let's dip our feet in," I say. This time it takes me several goes to open the gate. "Did you have lots of pool parties here?" asks Brandon, as he goes towards the water, pulls off his trainers and socks, and lowers his foot in. "Whoa. Colder than it looks."

"A few," I say. "But Mum and Dad had very strict rules. They were worried about someone drowning." I look away, to where the trampoline used to be.

"This must be hard for you," says Brandon. "The minute you want to leave, we'll go."

"Thanks. I'm OK for the moment." And I am. I'm here and I'm OK.

He sits on the edge of the pool with his legs in the water, the sleeves of his hoody pushed up to his elbow. It's difficult to take in that we're here, two worlds colliding.

"Once you get used to the temperature, this is quite pleasant," he says.

Slowly, squatting, I undo my laces, loosen first one canvas shoe, then the other, stand up and step out of them. Without either of us saying anything, I sit down next to Brandon, both legs pulled up. Gradually I hover them both over the pool, straining my stomach muscles.

"Go on," says Brandon, and I plunge them into the water together, gasping.

We swirl our feet about. I've hardly ever sat like this by a pool. The lure of the water was always too much, and I couldn't bear not being in it. "If I had a swimming costume with me, I might be tempted to swim," I say.

"You could strip off," says Brandon. He looks embarrassed. "I don't mean naked. Underwear. It's like a bikini, isn't it?"

Not really. I'm wearing lilac pants with a band of lace round the top. My bra is ... I hitch back the shoulder of my T-shirt. It's not my white-turned-grey one, but it's a bad clash with my pants: turquoise and white stripes. I want to get over my phobia – that's the most important thing. The pool is calm and clean, and I'm not panicking. The MessageHound stuff is over. Everything is OK.

"I'm doing it," I say. Before I can think too carefully, I remove my outer layers and run to the shallow end.

Brandon laughs as I lower myself into the water that reaches my thighs, squealing from the coldness.

"The new people are stingy with their pool heating."

"They're on holiday," calls Brandon. "They weren't expecting visitors."

If I wasn't wearing my underwear I would be doing this way more slowly, but to cover up my bra, I crouch down until my shoulders are immersed. "Oh my God," I shriek. "I can't feel my legs any more."

"Get swimming, then," calls Brandon.

"Aren't you coming in with me?"

"Nope. Too cold for me."

"Wimp."

I'm in the pool where Luisa died. The knowledge hits me in the throat. I breathe in and out deliberately loudly so I can keep it under control. My coordination is off-kilter for a few seconds. I've turned into my granny, who swam so slowly I could never understand why she didn't sink.

Do a length and get out. I face the house and push off against the smooth-tiled wall of the shallow end. With my neck extended and my head out of the water, I glide and twitch my legs enough to move forward. It feels unnatural so I lower my head into the water. It's a relief to sink into the world of dappled noise and refracted light. Without thinking about it, I've switched to front crawl, and I have the familiar sensation of being cut off from the real world. At the end of the pool, I lift my head to take a breath.

I've done it: one length in the pool.

Ahead, through the glass panels, there's the lawn and the patio area. In my flashbacks I'm often here, at the end of the pool, lifting my head towards the house like this. I see Luisa running. This afternoon there's no one there, but that doesn't stop my heart stumbling and my ribs pulling closer together.

I can't breathe.

twenty-eight

Yew Tree House, last summer

I'm swimming lengths, most of them underwater and in one breath, my favourite kind. As I lift my head at the end of a length and face the house, I see Luisa running across the grass towards me. She's trying to get my attention.

Afterwards, when the only sounds are the birds, a dog barking in the distance, and the thumping in my head, I stay hidden. I push my face into my knees and breathe in fumes of chlorine from my skin. It seeps into every part of my body.

I stay there but I don't know for how long. My brain is sludge and I can't process anything.

When I unfold myself and go outside, and see the red water and the lifeless body and the floating hair, Mum's there. She kicks off her sandals and jumps into the pool fully clothed and pulls Luisa to the side.

"Why didn't you do something?" she screams at me from the red water. There are soon police and other people. I see the gash on the side of Luisa's head, the way it looks like raw meat. Her puffy face. I know she's dead, but it's too big a thing to know. So I scream at her to wake up, and I can't stop.

twenty-nine

Now

I'm half out of the pool. Head on folded arms. Beached. My lungs are starved of oxygen and my heart's beating way too fast. The stuff that drips from my forehead is sweat, not water.

"Skye. Give me your hand."

I let Brandon pull me out of the pool, and I sit, trembling, letting the fear drain from me. I don't have the energy to care that he sees me this way or that I'm wearing mismatched old underwear.

"Was it a panic attack?" He wriggles out of his hoody and places it round me. "You'll warm up in a minute." He rubs my back vigorously and sits so close that he's in the patch of wetness that I've created around me.

We stay like that for what seems a long time. I let my body relax, bit by bit. Then he says, "There was a boy in the sixth form at my school who drowned on holiday in the hotel pool after taking a load of drugs."

He's trying to tell me he understands. "My sister wasn't into taking drugs," I say. "She started dealing at uni. Her boyfriend, Nico, was a supplier. It was about the money. She knew Dad had borrowed loads and couldn't pay it back. We were about to lose the house. She was about to lose her allowance . . . she liked nice things." The truth is a series of threads that have to be woven together to be understood. I've never tried to explain it this carefully to anyone before. "I think she liked the excitement of the dealing too. Perhaps in the beginning it was a laugh. She thought she could handle it. She was used to being in charge and things going her way. It was how she was."

My mouth is dry and my lips taste of chlorine. I huddle into my knees, like I did that day. "I told you I wasn't here when Luisa drowned, but I was. I was hiding in there." I point in the direction of the changing room. "She and Nico had got on the wrong side of a dealer in Hoathley because they were selling drugs on his turf. He came to the house to . . . talk to her." My stomach is folding in on itself. "It was my fault. I told him where we lived and I led him straight to her."

Afterwards, when I was interviewed by the police, I realized I'd blurted our address to the dealer about a week before Luisa died. I was proud to be part of what

I thought was Luisa's nutrition business, handing over envelopes a few times. I was supposed to be handing over a pink envelope to a woman sitting on her own on a certain bench in a park, but when I got there, she was with someone else, a man. He asked me where Luisa ran her business from. I wasn't supposed to talk to clients, but Luisa was in the car park, on her mobile, and I knew I'd have to wait for her call to be over. I told him Pitford. He said, "Near the farm shop?" He was smiley, polite, so I said *Next door. Yew Tree House.* As I said it I thought *Yew Tree House Nutrition* had a good ring to it, but when I returned to the car, Luisa was still on the phone and I forgot to suggest it to her.

"You didn't know what you were doing," says Brandon.

I shake my head. I didn't, but I was so, so stupid. Too trusting. The hoody is soft against my skin, and it smells of Brandon. I could stop talking now, but it wouldn't be the whole truth.

"Luisa and the Hoathley dealer had an argument," I say. "I was watching from a crack in the doorway."

Keep going, I tell myself. *Get to the end.*

"The police told me that he punched her. I was hiding by then but I heard her scream." I shudder as I remember the scream that sliced through my brain, how the breath caught in my throat. "She lost her balance from the punch and tripped. Hit her head and fell into the pool unconscious. She drowned in the water." I allow a split-second pause before I irrevocably change Brandon's view of me. "She drowned because I didn't save her. I was there and I didn't save her." My voice shakes. "Luisa had told me to hide and I didn't know if the man had gone or not, but those are excuses. I was paralysed by shock . . . fear. I sort of froze and I don't know why."

"Oh," says Brandon, or that's what it sounds like. A startled *oh*. We sit in silence while I imagine what's going on in his head.

"There are always things people wish they'd done or not done," he says at last. "My dad got all this stuff in his head about living too near pylons, and my mum said they should have taken my brother for treatment somewhere else."

It's as if he's deliberately misheard everything I've just told him, too embarrassed to confront the reality. "But you don't get it," I say. "There is something I could have done which would have a hundred per cent saved my sister." I stand up. "What you're talking about is different. Why are you pretending it's the same?"

"I was just—"

I can't bear his placatory tone. "Don't. I don't need anyone feeling sorry for me."

"Skye, you're—"

"What?" I'm almost shouting. I want to hear what he's really saying under all his don't-worry chat. "I'm what?"

Brandon's forehead creases. "You're getting it out of proportion."

But I know what I saw. I saw shock in his eyes when I told him. He doesn't want to upset me – it's easier to soothe me until he's safely away from me. "So answer this," I say. "If you could have saved your brother with some sort of transplant even though there was a relatively big risk to your own health, would you have gone through with it?" I ask.

"Course," says Brandon. "I'd have done everything I could to save him."

"You see," I say. "That's what I'm talking about."

"But—"

"You said it. You'd have done everything you could to save him."

"Oh, for God's sake," says Brandon. He shakes his head and stands up. Looks towards the gate. I bet he wishes he could walk away and leave me here. I've disappointed him. Disgusted him.

At least he knows the real me now. There's a relief in being open.

I take off his hoody and hand it to him. "We should go."

He takes the hoody. "Aren't you cold?"

"I'm OK," I say, and I will be. I just need to get back to Morley Hill, survive one more night and go home. I've had enough of teams and talking, and being Yellow. I reach down to pick up my clothes, and I ache all over. Weariness has infiltrated every cell of my body. Yanking my clothes on takes some time because the material sticks to my damp skin. When I look down, I see I have embarrassing wet patches on my shorts and T-shirt from my pants and bra. I wish I still had Brandon's hoody to cover them up, but I'm not going to ask for it back again. Brandon has his socks and trainers on already, and is waiting by the gate. I squeeze the excess water from my hair and shove my feet into my canvas shoes. I walk a few paces before stopping to tie the laces. It takes ages because my fingers are stiff.

We walk through the pool gate in silence and I close it firmly so it click–clacks loudly. The noise reverberates round the garden and in my head.

When we reach the wall, Brandon says, "Are we going to leave the gate unbolted?" He's quiet, already detached from me.

I shake my head. The family will freak if they see someone's opened the gate from the inside, but it's set within the wall, which makes it too difficult to climb over. I look up at the closest tree. "I think I can swing on to the wall and jump off it into the field," I say.

Brandon looks surprised but says, "OK." He squeezes through to the field and disappears.

I do the bolts and return the wheelbarrow to where it was, up against the gate. Moving slowly, I heave myself up to the first fork in the tree. My body isn't back to normal and my clothes are uncomfortable but I can't think about them. Or Brandon.

Keep climbing. Up. Up.

I seize the branch that should help me reach the wall. One. Two. Three. *Swing.* My balance is off but it's enough to propel myself from the wall into the field. I land on both feet in the tufty grass, crouching. Shocked I made it without hurting myself.

Brandon's there. "All right?"

I nod, and he says, "Good. Let's go."

There are cows in this field, but neither of us feels like joking about them as we make our way back to the track.

"So it's over, then," says Brandon at the bus stop, when we see the bus in the distance. I know he's talking about the messages, and maybe he's referring to my swimming phobia too, but I'm sure he's including us in there somewhere.

"Yes," I say. "Toby didn't set out to properly frighten me. He got carried away."

Brandon nods, but I wonder if he's really listening. He looks out at the hedges and fences, the estates of newly built houses. Kids on bikes. While we wait for the second bus in Hoathley, he plays with his phone. I think about the long shower that I'll have when I get back to my room. Removing the smell of chlorine takes time and loads of shower gel.

As we walk through the fields, I say, "Thanks for coming with me. I'm sorry it was so intense."

"You're welcome," says Brandon. He's being formal with me now. I don't blame him.

By tomorrow evening I'll be home again. I won't wind Mum up, I'll answer Dad's endless questions about the activities, and I'll pretend to be interested and wildly jealous of all the things that Oscar's been doing while I haven't been there. And all the time, I'll be trying to forget about Brandon.

We climb over the final gate, into the campfire area, and say a hurried goodbye before he peels off to his accommodation block.

I continue to my room. The others aren't there but, typically, Fay's already packed her things. She's moved her suitcase from the shelf on to her bed. The biohazard of a rabbit lies on her pillow. Danielle's stuff, like mine, is all over the place. Still cold from the pool, I climb under the duvet and pull the pillow over my head for five minutes before I have a shower.

The door bursts open and I hear Danielle say, "Skye, where've you been? Are you ill?"

I pull the pillow from my head and roll on to my side. "Out and about. Just having a nap."

"Have you seen Fay?"

"No. Why?"

"She's missing. I need to find her."

I flop on to my stomach again, and press my forehead against my folded arms. "She's probably gone off somewhere with Joe, and will be back for dinner."

"Joe says he hasn't seen her for ages."

Lifting my head slightly so that Danielle can hear me, I say, "What's the big fuss? Why d'you need her?"

"My tablets are missing too."

thirty

The little hinged tin is missing, along with its contents: white chalky tablets and the cylindrical pills with the pale blue coating.

"I had them this morning," says Danielle. "Someone has definitely come in here and taken them." She fixes me with an accusing look. "You didn't tell anyone about them, did you?"

I'm sitting up against my pillow. I should have gone straight to the shower when I came back. My clothes are rank, and my hair is stiff and knotty.

"No."

"You and Fay are the only people who knew I had them. Fay asked me what I kept in the tin, and I told her the tablets were for my migraines."

Seriously? Migraine medication would come in bubble packs, not loose in little tins. Fay, aspiring medic, would know that.

"Why would Fay take them? Maybe a cleaner found them and handed them in."

Danielle bites her lip. "Fay's going to get me into trouble, I know she is. And does this room look as if it's been cleaned since we've been here?"

The last time I saw Fay was on the minibus, coming back from the tower, where she was cosied up to Joe. "Perhaps she told Joe and he's behind it. Teaching you a lesson. You know what he's like."

"I've spoken to Joe. Said I was looking for Fay but not what it was about. He said she told him that she wanted some time on her own this afternoon to pack. I've been searching for ages. Will you come with me one last time before dinner? I need to do a circuit round the village too."

"Can I have a shower first?"

"No. You look fine. Wait. Have you been swimming? Your hair's damp. I thought you had a phobia."

"I. . ." It's too complicated. I grab some dry clothes from my suitcase and go into the bathroom. "Give me a few seconds to get changed into something else."

I trail after Danielle as we look in the common room, the hall where the Reds do their music, reception, the main dining room, the yellow dining room, the games room and the swimming pool. As I sense her growing panic about the missing tablets, I suggest we walk down the paths in the grounds, including the one round the lake.

We stop by the boathouse for her to light a cigarette. The boating sessions are over for the day, so there are no instructors there. "I'm going to be in massive trouble," says Danielle. She leans against the wall, next to the big closed wooden doors that face on to the lake, and shuts her eyes.

I push open the side door to the boathouse and step inside. The only two windows it has are semi-covered in wet green mould and the light doesn't work, so it's gloomy and not the sort of place you'd want to hang around in. I walk past the rail of life jackets and the open wire cubbyholes for people to leave their shoes in. The kayaks are in their racking slots, by the big wooden doors. To the other side, there's a desktop with boat parts and repair equipment on it, a bashed metal filing cabinet, and right at the back, a kitchen area with gross stains on the wall. There's a laminated hygiene certificate propped up on the work surface and someone has scrawled in marker pen *You must be joking.*

"She's not in here," I shout.

When Danielle's finished her cigarette and tossed the end into the lake, we carry on. The other buildings are locked. We try to remember what we last saw Fay wearing and decide it was a T-shirt with a koala on the front and shorts, possibly pink, and we ask a few Reds who are dotted about, practising their multiple-part harmonies, if they've seen her. No one has.

"We have to try the village," says Danielle. "Before dinner."

"What's the time?"

Danielle looks at her phone but doesn't tell me. "We'll be five minutes."

"Let's wait until dinner. See if she turns up." I'm thinking of a five-minute shower. Of clean hair and skin that doesn't remind me of the pool at Yew Tree House.

Danielle drags me by the arm. "Come on." She hauls me along the path towards the reception building. "We're going to find her sitting on a bench by the war memorial." She says it without conviction.

"Reception are never going to let us out at this time," I say. "We'll have to go the back way, over the fields."

"Have you done this before – with Brandon?" She winks. I hate that wink.

"That orienteering thing – remember?" I head towards the gate.

"This is a really long way round," Danielle grumbles as we reach the stile at the other side of the first field. "Hey, you don't have Fay's mobile number, do you?"

"No, and she's probably already packed her phone." I think of the suitcase on the neatly made bed. The rabbit on the pillow. How when I went into the bathroom to change clothes, none of her washbag stuff was there. She must have packed that too. Why did she do that? Surely she'd need it for tonight and tomorrow morning. Why does that make me uneasy?

"Danielle, we have to go back to the room."

"What?"

"We have to check Fay's suitcase." I turn and jog back along the footpath, gesturing for Danielle to follow. "Hurry," I shout as I break into a run. "I'll explain when we get there."

The quietness of our room is unnerving. My unease balloons into dread. I touch the tough meshed surface of the burgundy-coloured suitcase, feel for the zip, and trace it to the end. "Fay packed as if she'd already left," I say. "That's a bad sign."

The zip makes a brisk whirring sound as I undo it. Slowly, I lift the lid. There, on top of folded clothes, is a sheet of folded white paper.

Unfolding the note, I scan its contents before I read it properly. My legs weaken. Danielle peers over my shoulder and I hold it out for her so she can see it better. It's not the sort of letter you read out loud.

Mum,

I can't live with the shame.

I'm sorry for everything.

Fay x

Danielle buries her face into her hands.

My mind floods with an image of Luisa floating face down in the pool. "We have to find Pippa," I say.

In the yellow dining room, most people have already

served themselves and sat down. Pippa is at the back of the queue. From the way we've burst in, she can see that something is wrong. I hand her the letter, and let Danielle explain about the tablets. A hush comes over the dining room, followed by frenzied speculation from everyone, especially when they see Danielle sobbing. I sense Brandon looking at me, wanting to know what's going on, but when Pippa asks me and Danielle to go with her, I follow without catching his eye.

"We'll go to the main office in the reception building," says Pippa as soon as we're in the corridor with the door closed behind us. "We have a set procedure for this sort of thing. I'll contact the police and our centre director. All the instructors will come in and help in the search. Please don't worry."

I nod slightly. She sounds as if she knows what she's doing.

"Please! Wait." Joe is running after us. "What's happened? If it's about Fay, I need to know."

"D'you know where she is?" Pippa asks.

Joe shakes his head. "That piece of paper? Was it . . . ?"

"I know you and Fay are close," says Pippa. "When did you last see her?"

"This afternoon, after swimming. She wanted to pack. What's happened?"

"We think," Pippa speaks slowly, "but we're not certain, that Fay may have taken an overdose, but we don't know where she is."

Joe scrunches his eyes shut. "No. Not again."

Is it just coincidence that this is happening a second time to him?

"This must be very hard for you," says Pippa, "but I need your help. Has she phoned you this afternoon? Or texted?"

He shakes his head. "No, I haven't heard from her at all." He sounds utterly convincing, but I don't trust him.

"Can you check your phone?" I ask, in case Pippa isn't going to.

"She hasn't been in touch," insists Joe, but he reaches into the pocket of his shorts to pull out his phone. He looks at the screen. "No messages." He unlocks the phone and shows Pippa. "Nothing from her today. She knows I don't like to use my mobile much."

The message he sent Fay the other night will be logged somewhere: *Dream of angels Fay x*. The choice of words seems chilling now.

"Thanks, Joe," says Pippa. "Come with us to the office. You can give the police a statement too."

"Sure," says Joe. "I'll help in any way I can."

Before he returns the phone to his pocket, I catch a glimpse of his home screen. It's a photo of him and Fay. She has something round her neck that's similar to something I've seen before, but not on her. A triangular piece of driftwood that has a little symbol on it. It's pretty much identical to the one I saw on the photo of his ex-girlfriend. What disturbs me most, though, is that their glazed expressions are identical too.

thirty-one

Danielle, Joe and I sit in silence while Pippa makes phone calls. I can't sit still though. I cross and uncross my legs, and bite the inside of my cheek. The whole of Yellow Group should be out looking for Fay. Someone should already be checking every inch of this place. I don't understand why the police haven't arrived yet, why I can't hear their sirens. When the centre director arrives, he asks us what we know, takes notes, and says we should wait in the office while he and Pippa brief the instructors in the staffroom.

As soon as we're on our own, Danielle says, "This is going to hit my dad hard."

"You are unbelievably selfish," says Joe. He stands up

and walks to a noticeboard. "You should be thinking about Fay. And what you've done." He has his back to us, head bowed, rubbing his temples, but I swear he's reading a letter pinned on to the board.

So much about him troubles me. The photos of Kyra and Fay with similar necklaces and expressions, his lies about Kyra's birthday, his creepy behaviour. Yet it's insubstantial, nothing I could tell the police without sounding flaky.

I stand up too. I need to move properly, to do something. Through the window I see a couple of instructors arrive on their bicycles, making their way to the bike rack. They take their time locking their bikes. They're chatting. I want to scream at them to hurry up. Fay needs to be found; time's running out.

Think. Think. Did Fay leave any clues about where she would go? What was going through her mind?

The instructors move out of sight and I pace the room, ending up at the other window that looks out over the grounds. I lean my head against the window, craving the coolness of it on my forehead. The signpost to the different parts of Morley Hill is visible from here. *Campfire Area. High-Ropes Course. Swimming Pool . . . The Lake.* Fay's words from the day we kayaked on the lake float into my head: *I'd like to live on an island like that. Far away from everyone.*

She could be there on the island. She'd have kayaked over. It wouldn't have taken long. It's private. A place she liked the look of. People wouldn't have noticed because there are often kayakers on the lake.

"I'll be back in a minute," I say to Joe and Danielle.

Danielle nods, but Joe stands up. "Where are you going? You have to stay here. That guy told you to stay here."

I ignore him, leave the room, and bolt to the staffroom. The instructors who I saw by the bike rack are at the door.

"Please," I pant. "I need to talk to Pippa urgently. I have an idea about where to search for Fay."

They look at me, then each other with surprise, as if they didn't think anyone else but Morley Hill staff knew that Fay was missing.

"Er. OK," says one. He pokes his head into the staffroom. "She's on the phone." He looks in my direction again. "What's your idea, then?"

"The island in the lake," I say.

"Yeah, OK. No probs. I'm sure we'll be searching the whole grounds. We need a briefing first."

"You need to get a move on," I say. My voice cracks. "Can I speak to the centre director?"

The instructor looks blank. "The who?"

"The tall man." *Great description, Skye.* I can't remember his name or what he was wearing. A grey T-shirt with a white logo on it? I shake my head. I can't waste any more time. "Forget it. Tell Pippa as soon as she's off the phone."

"All right." But I barely hear his answer because I'm on my way to the boathouse.

*

The only place I failed to look in the boathouse earlier was the racking, to see if any of the boats were missing. I yank the big doors at the front. They creak open, gather momentum, swing back and bang loudly against the building. One of the wooden slots is empty, damp from where a boat out of the water has been stored at the end of the afternoon's session, and then removed.

Either Fay took it, one of the other water-sports instructors took it, or the centre was always one boat short of a full racking and the shelving is wet because boats have been rearranged. I'm going with the theory that Fay took it, and I can't wait for anyone else to act on it. Too much time has already spun by with note-taking and briefing.

All the kayaks are singles. If Fay's on the island, I'll have to either persuade her to paddle back alongside me in her boat if she's capable, or wait for help from the instructors. I haul out the closest one to me and set it on the ground, before running to snatch a life jacket and paddle from inside the boathouse.

With my life jacket on, I lug the boat on its side to the water's edge without dropping it, the paddle and my flip-flops tucked inside. For a few seconds I contemplate using the jetty, but I opt for dragging the kayak into the lake. Before the water reaches the hem of my shorts, I hold the kayak as steady as I can and lift one leg up and into the boat. Gradually I ease the rest of my body in. I'm in, but my paddle is stuck under the seats. I yank it and the boat lurches.

Keep steady. Breathe deeply.

The water is darker and colder than the other morning, and smells of damp caves, or a cellar where bad things happen.

My technique's bad but I'm moving forward in the right direction, and the boat is mostly stable. The further out I go, the quieter everything is. In the distance there's the mocking squawks of birds; closer, the slap and drag of water against my paddle.

My shoulders stiffen and burn from the effort of paddling as fast as I can. I keep my eyes on the chunk of land ahead, with the trees that stick out like a bad haircut. Pulling the paddle through the water becomes harder and harder. At last, I see the lake changing colour, becoming lighter, and I'm in shallower water. A sign set back from the shore says *Keep Out. Nature Reserve.* I try and touch the bottom with my paddle. I can but it's still too deep to jump out. Another five strokes, and I can't wait any longer. I swing one leg out, rock the boat too far and that's it. I'm in the water. It's shallow enough to stand up in but it's still deep enough to drown in, I'm soaked up to my waist, and the weight of the water is dragging my shorts down.

But I made it.

"Fay!" I shout. "Fay, it's Skye!"

The kayak doesn't want to be dragged up the gravelly shore of the island. It wants to bob about on the water or drift back into the middle of the lake. I push it instead, imagining the chaotic pattern of jagged scratches that I'm creating underneath. Eventually I wedge it far enough up the beach to stop it sliding back, and dump my thick life jacket on top.

Heavy raindrops land like small paint splatters on and around me and the sky darkens. Any moment now there's going to be a full-scale downpour.

The island looked tiny from across the water. Now it seems like an enormous jungle, the size of the Mulligans' largest field. If Fay took out a boat, it'll be here somewhere because it wasn't floating about on the lake. I find my flip-flops but they're uncomfortable with my feet being so wet, so I carry them. Now I think about it, Fay's bound to have hidden her kayak further round the island where it can't be seen from the boathouse. I should have kayaked around the island first instead of being in too much of a rush to reach the shore.

I hobble along the gravelly beach. As the shoreline curves, I see a large tree has fallen across the beach and I put a spurt on. The thick trunk is the perfect place to hide behind.

The deluge comes as I'm almost there. Within seconds I'm soaked and freezing, and the lake water and sky merge to the same blurry grey. The fallen trunk is so big I have to clamber over it. Fragments of bark and moss stick to me. As I jump down on to the stony beach the other side, I see a kayak sticking out of some bushes.

"Fay!" I scream as I fall upon the boat. "Faaaaaaaay!" The boat's empty apart from the paddle. She must have gone into the woods. I run along the mass of nettles and brambles, scanning for a path or the place where they've been trampled. When I spot a slight opening, I drop my flip-flops to the ground and wriggle my feet into them. The stones give way to uneven, spongy ground as I take careful steps into the woods. Rain pounds down in occasional gaps in the trees and gushes over me when I dislodge the puddles that have collected on large leaves. In the first few metres I'm stung by nettles multiple times, and jump at the sound of something small scuttling nearby, but I push on through the undergrowth. My eyes adjust to the darkness, and I follow the path of flattened vegetation, my wet feet slipping on flip-flops that have no grip either.

Wet shorts rub my thighs, and my exposed skin is attacked by nettles, thorns and clouds of insects. I'm scared I'll stumble over Fay's body or brush against it, hanging from a tree. Of what she'll look like. Whether she'll be alive or dead.

"Please tell me where you are," I say in a voice she'll never hear over the sound of the rain.

In this damp and shaded world, there are uncurling ferns, new shoots and dried, fallen leaves, now turning soggy, and rotting berries. Life and decay going on at the same time. I squeeze between two dense bushes and I see pink. Fay's shorts. She's lying on her dad's old swimming towel, on her side, in shorts, koala T-shirt and sopping wet canvas shoes. Her legs and arms, like mine, are covered in scratches and a rash of nettle stings. She's asleep, unconscious or dead.

"Fay? Fay! Can you hear me?" I roll her on to her back and tap her cheeks, like I've seen people do in films. "Please. Open your eyes." It's hard to tell if she's breathing. Her face is pale, but not super-white. Her chest is still and I can't find a pulse. I swallow down my panic and hold my hand up near her mouth. There's a tiny tickle against it. Shallow breathing.

"I'm going to lift you up," I say as I slip one arm under her cold neck and the other under her knees and lift her up. She weighs less than my brother, but I'm not sure how long I'll be able to hold her. Her body is floppy, and her head falls back.

"It's OK, Fay," I say. "I'm going to help you." As I stagger through the undergrowth with her, I can't keep the branches from hitting me or the dusty bits from the trees from getting in my eyes and hair. Muscles, joints, everything in my upper body is crunched with the strain of carrying her.

"We're nearly at the lake," I say. "You're going to be OK." I stumble out of the woods into the rain and sink to my knees on the stony beach, unable to carry Fay any further. The moment I lay her down, she moans.

I hover over her face. "Fay? Can you hear me? It's Skye."

Her eyelids flutter but fail to open fully. "Don't. . ." she croaks. "Don't leave me."

"I won't. I promise." Water drips from my soaking clothes, and I shiver. It's bad enough for me, but Fay's going to worsen quickly in these conditions.

It would be impossible for me to paddle back to the shore with her draped over a kayak. How long will it be before someone comes over to the island to help us? We're too far round for anyone to see us easily. I'll have to go back to my kayak, find my neon-orange life jacket, and wave it for attention. The quickest way is over the tree, but it'll be difficult with Fay. I stand to assess the tree, to work out if I can lift her over, or if I should go on my own, despite my promise not to leave her. It might be the only way I can do this. There's a movement the other side of the tree trunk. I rush towards it. Please let it be a person. Someone who can get Fay help faster than I can. It's a figure in a black wetsuit, hair slicked back, jogging along the beach. "Over here!" I shout into the wind and rain. "Hurry."

Relief switches to gut-wringing fear when I see who it is: Joe.

thirty-two

"I don't know why you're looking so terrified," says Joe as he leaps on to the tree with ease and jumps down. "Did I make you jump?"

I lumber backwards in a futile attempt to block Fay from his view.

He comes closer. "How is she?" he asks. He touches his hair to see how wet it is.

"Leave her alone," I say.

Joe peers round me as my heart thuds, sees enough, then backs off. "Leave her alone?" he says. He looks amused. "That's precisely what I'm doing."

"Where are the instructors? Pippa?" I look past him, willing someone else to be coming along the beach.

He glances up at the sky. "Ah, look, the rain's easing off a bit."

"Where's everyone else, Joe?" I ask slowly.

"I'm the search party for the island."

I take a step back. "What?"

"I said I'd cover the island with the water-sports instructor, Tim. Remember Tim? He rescued you when you capsized."

I speak as calmly as I can. "So where's Tim?"

"He's not here yet. Pippa says he lives quite far away. I thought I'd come across first. I'm a Level 1 kayak coach at my club. Unfortunately I don't have any phone signal here. And I don't think your phone is working. Is it?"

Alarm ricochets through me. He lies and manipulates so smoothly. "You knew she was here all along, didn't you?"

"We discussed it, yes. It seemed a tranquil place to start the next stage of her process."

Her process? I'd like to laugh in his face, but I have to be careful. The heavy thuds of my heart are a measure of what I think he's capable of.

"What are you talking about?" I say, crouching next to Fay to put her into the recovery position in case she vomits. If he's spouting his strange theories, then he's less likely to concern himself with what I'm doing.

"The universe demands balance, yes?"

Time slows into a heightened version of reality as I watch Joe settle himself on the wet gravel, leaning back on his elbows, his legs stretched out. It could be a mood shot for an advert. A wetsuit-clad surfer dude deep in thought on a wild, secluded beach in the rain, with woods in the background. He picks up a stone, larger than most of the others, and turns it over in his hands, inspecting the surface.

I rearrange Fay slightly, and pull away the sharper-looking pebbles underneath her to make her more comfortable.

"If the balance is disturbed, things go wrong," says Joe. "Look at our twisted world. Too much food and consumerism for some, while others starve. For every action there has to be an equal and opposite reaction. It's Newton's undisputed third law of motion."

I need to grab my life jacket and attract attention. Now. But I can't leave Fay with Joe. I have no choice. As I lift her up, as gently as I can, Joe jogs over.

"What are you doing?"

I ignore him.

He blocks my way, standing so close I can smell wetsuit with a base note of sweat. "You're not getting this, are you?" he says, peering at her face. "Fay needed help to right the wrong she did by causing her father to crash his car. In order to purify each and every one of us. She was full of shame and darkness. There was a solution – cleansing herself by destroying the shame."

"By taking an overdose?" I walk round him, Fay heavy now in my arms, and he lets me.

So he's not going to do anything to help Fay, but restraining me isn't part of his plan. Not at the moment.

"That was the route she chose herself," says Joe.

I'll lay Fay on the fallen tree trunk, at the lowest point, climb over first, then pick her up. Joe follows me.

"I didn't force her to do this. I wasn't anywhere near her when she took those pills." It's the first time he's sounded defensive.

"But she did it for you."

"She did it for the universe. It's not death. Fay will exist beyond time. She's learning and growing."

I stare at him and out of the corner of my eye I notice movement out on the lake. Kayaks! Help's on the way. I open my mouth to scream but close it again in stunned disbelief when I realize. There's no one in the kayaks.

"A strong offshore wind," says Joe, with a pretend-sad face. "Too bad we didn't tie up our boats properly in our panic to find Fay."

He's by her boat now. Almost in one fluid movement, he pulls out the paddle and throws it into the nettles. He picks up the kayak and carries it to the shore, where he shoves it as hard as he can with both hands into the lake. "Don't worry, Fay doesn't need it," he calls up the beach to me.

Fay makes a gurgling noise. Her eyes are shut, her body unresponsive again, and I hurry on, toes grimly gripping my flip-flops, towards the tree, even though there's no life jacket for me to wave on the other side – it's out on the lake, inside my kayak.

It would take hardly any effort for Joe, taller and stronger than me, to carry Fay over this massive trunk. I have to balance her on it long enough for me to clamber over myself. Twice she almost slides off. Her face is greyish and clammy, her partially open lips horribly dry in contrast.

"There's no point dragging her round the island," calls Joe, walking slowly back up the beach towards me. "She's not got long."

I try to imagine he's not there, only a couple of metres away, smirking. It half works until he starts talking again. "I liked you," he says. "And you know what? I could see that you were full of shame and self-loathing. I would have helped you." He comes a little closer, and speaks in a softer voice. "I was wrong. You're not worth saving. You're trouble. That's why I chose to help Fay. She proved herself to me. She has what it takes."

So I'm not as needy and vulnerable as he'd have liked? That backhanded compliment gives me the boost of strength I need to haul myself over the tree. But I cry out as I rip off the scab from when I fell on the paving slabs by the pool on the first day.

"You're going against Fay's wishes – I hope you'll be able to live with yourself knowing that," says Joe, jumping on to the tree trunk, assuming his favourite position up on high.

"She was under your influence," I spit at him as I position myself to pick up Fay. "Like Kyra, I expect."

"I miss Kyra," says Joe. He jumps down, slamming into my shoulder, almost knocking me over.

Breathe in through the nose. Out through the mouth.

"Unfortunately she took the wrong path. The path of shame. I didn't want her to move on. It broke my heart but the universe demanded it."

I grip Fay close to me, over-tightly because I'm shaking so much it's hard to control my limbs. But I have to ask. "A naked photo – that was the path of shame? Or was it because she tried to break up with you?"

Joe bends down to pick up a large pebble. My shaking becomes more violent and I keep walking, praying he's not going to throw it at my head. There's a loud splash and I assume he's hurled it in the lake. He shouts at my back. "She made the wrong choice. She chose someone else over me, and he let her down."

There. I can see the boathouse, but – I squint and move closer to the shore – there's no one in sight.

"Help!" I scream. "*Hellllp!*"

I hear Joe's footsteps, steady on the shingle. "Shout all you like," he says. "Your voice won't carry across the lake, and anyway, the focus of the search is in the village right now. It'll give Fay the last bit of time she needs." He glances at her, and she's suddenly so heavy that I have to lay her down, right there on the damp stones.

I'm almost too stiff and tired to place her in the recovery position, but I do it, forcing away a surge of frustration towards her, at allowing herself to fall under

Joe's spell. Her hand reaches feebly for mine, and I know I'll do anything to save her.

"All right, you win," I say to Joe. "I'll make her comfortable, and wait."

Joe smiles and I have to look away. "Good girl. I knew you'd see sense sooner or later."

I want to punch him with all my remaining strength, but I'm going to need it very soon.

"She wanted to die on her dad's towel," I say. "She brought it all the way here and I left it in the woods. It's not far away. Please would you get it for her?"

"You know where it is; you get it." His eyes are narrowed.

I give a long sigh. "I'm exhausted, Joe. Please. Let's respect Fay's last wishes."

He thinks for a moment. "Where is it?"

I tell him roughly – he'll see the trampled vegetation where Fay entered the woods for himself, so there's no point going for wild lies, even though I need as much of a head start as I can get.

It's agony to stay still until he disappears from sight behind the fallen tree, but then I flick off my flip-flops, yank off Fay's shoes and scoop her up.

"I'm going to swim across the lake with you," I whisper in her ear.

The first touch of the water round my ankles is a relief. It's cool against my stings. As I wade in deeper, as fast as I can without making too many splashing noises, I'm overwhelmed by the dread of a panic attack. I remind myself I'm wet already from the rain. That I can do this.

"Here we go, Fay. It's going to be OK." I float her in the water and grip under her chin with one hand. With my spare arm I scull. The best stroke for my legs, trying to keep clear of Fay, is a mixture of kicking and breaststroke.

I fight the fatigue that's already in my muscles and pretend I'm swimming in front of a home crowd at the club. Every metre of water between us and Joe counts. I've seen him in the pool. He's not a bad swimmer. He can leap easily across the tree and enter the water further along the beach to give him an advantage,

Swooshing and swishing fill my ears as I lean my head back, the eerie amplified language of water. I smell chlorine, lingering on my skin from earlier. Droplets splash into my eyes. I close them and see blood. Blood everywhere. The water in my eyes is no longer lake water but salty, blood-red tears for my beautiful, sweet, stupid drug-dealing sister who died on her own when I was there, so close to her.

After a while, I open my eyes, check my direction and look at Fay's face. Her lips are a bluish colour.

I let the anger that surges within me give my muscles some power. There are so many people to be angry at, including myself.

"Hang on," I whisper to Fay. "Please hang on."

Her face is white. My brain superimposes Luisa's face, puffy with an open wound.

Where's Tim? I fantasize about him coming by with a motor boat and lifting us out of the water.

Rain drizzles down endlessly. The next time I raise my head, I miss a breath. Joe's in the water, swimming front crawl. I pull Fay closer to me and double my effort. Faster. Stronger. Every muscle in my body is shredding apart. My lungs are bulging. The water is no longer cold but warm like bath water. I'm going to be sick. It rises and I turn my head. Swim on for several agonizing strokes to avoid it; then two whole seconds are wasted as I tread water and gasp.

Joe's gaining. It's inevitable.

"We're nearly there, Fay," I say through a mouth that's dry and foul-tasting. But maybe I think the words instead, or say the wrong ones. I can no longer lift my head and when the movement of the water changes, I sense rather than see that Joe has almost caught up with me.

Noise drifts towards me but other people's words don't make much sense either. *We're coming. Hang on.*

"*Help!*" I yell inside my head.

Joe's alongside. Out of breath. Weaker than I thought. "Skye, let me take her." I can't work out what he means.

His arms reach out and I lurch away, desperate to keep my head above water, gasping. I lift up Fay with the last of my energy. So this is what drowning's like. Silent because there's not enough air to shout.

More movement in the water. I still have hold of Fay. I see Luisa's lifeless, floating body next to us.

Shallow water. My feet touch the bottom.

Strong hands drag me and Fay out of the water. I've no idea whose. It's hard to stand upright so I lie down on the wet grass. I hear my gulpy, raspy breathing. I smell the disgusting boathouse towel. Feel its scratchy comfort. I see Fay being put on a stretcher. Next time I open my eyes there's the green uniform of a paramedic above me. Or maybe a traffic warden. No, definitely a paramedic.

"Fay?" I whisper, as the paramedic helps me to my feet and replaces the towel with a blanket. My mouth is dry and my throat hurts.

"On her way to hospital, my love. She's in good hands now."

I'd like to ask if Fay's going to live, but it's probably too early to tell, and my head is swirling and blackness is closing in.

When I wake up the rain has stopped, I'm on my side and I have a tight band round my arm that's becoming looser. "Blood pressure returning to normal," someone says, and there's the ear-startling sound of Velcro being pulled apart, followed by a new lightness in my arm. Through the blanket, I feel a firm hand on my back. "You're OK, my lovely. You fainted and we're going to keep an eye on you. Just lie there a moment and let the wooziness pass."

I give the tiniest of nods, and the hand on my back pats me in acknowledgement.

I hear Joe's voice next. "When we realized the kayaks

had drifted off, we didn't know what to do. We knew time was running out for Fay and we didn't have phones. I thought I'd brought mine but I must have left it in the main office."

Pippa's voice says, "Very brave of you to swim."

"Because Skye was the stronger swimmer, I told her that she should swim with Fay, and I'd swim beside them as backup."

How can he say these things?

I open my mouth to speak but cough. Lake water spews out of my mouth into a bowl that's being held in front of me. Someone holds back my hair. Now there's a hand on my shoulder. Tissues wipe my face.

"How did you know Skye was the stronger swimmer?" That's Brandon. "You'd never seen her swim before."

I want to hug Brandon. To hug him fiercely and feel his strong arms around me too. Being upset with him earlier seems a long time ago. He was shocked by what I told him, but maybe he wasn't as disgusted by me as I thought he should have been. Perhaps he could see that I was capable of more. That if I was given a second chance to save someone, I wouldn't hesitate.

"Maybe Skye told me she was a good swimmer. I don't remember the details," says Joe.

"I don't understand why your kayak drifted off," says Brandon. "You're a coach. I'd have thought you'd know how to secure it properly."

"Mate, you weren't there. It was a crisis situation." He

255

says something in a lower voice, and Pippa says, "Yes, of course. Could someone get Joe a cup of tea? Brandon, let's not bombard him with questions until he's had a chance to recover."

Let me speak. But when my eyes are open the dizziness takes my breath away. I feel myself falling back into the darkness and the conversations around me reduce to a murmur and then nothing.

Pippa's voice again. Loud, and possibly on the phone, telling someone that the paramedic reckoned Fay had received treatment in the nick of time, that she'd almost certainly make a good recovery.

Another conversation drifts towards me.

"We spoke earlier. I'm the centre director. I'd like to thank you, young man, for what you've done this evening."

"It's a pleasure, sir. My last girlfriend committed suicide last summer and I was determined it wasn't going to happen again. Fay and I are very close. Is there any chance of going to see her in the hospital?"

I snap my eyes open. It's an effort to sit up. "He. . ." I begin but my voice is a fraction of a whisper. I've lost my voice from shouting for help.

The paramedic is beside me. "Up you get. There you go. Let's sit you on the bench now."

I clutch my throat.

"Sore throat? I'll get you something for that," says the paramedic.

"Skye," says Pippa. "You and Joe really should have waited for Tim before going across to the island, but we're immensely grateful to you both."

Everyone swivels to look at me. There are far more people here than I realized. I look for Brandon, and can't see him. Where is he?

My eyes land on Joe, standing with a blanket round him. A mug of tea in his hands. He looks straight at me, a twitch of a smile at his mouth. "Feeling better, Skye?"

Does he think I'm too scared of him to speak out? The paramedic hands me some tea. My hands shake as I bring it to my mouth, mostly through rage and frustration. The hot liquid is soothing beyond anything I've experienced.

"We did a good job, you and me, didn't we?" says Joe.

"Lies," I say. It sounds like more of a regular whisper.

"Sorry?" asks Pippa. I beckon her over to me. Urgently. But Joe speaks first and distracts her. "We found Fay lying in the woods," he says. "With her dad's old towel."

Everyone's going to believe his version over mine.

The mention of the towel distracts people. Someone says Tim should kayak over and get it for Fay if it's that important to her.

In the middle of this discussion, Brandon appears, out of breath and waving some paper.

"You've got to..." he says, charging straight into the middle of everyone, bending momentarily to catch his breath before continuing. "You've got to see something."

"Brandon?" says Pippa. "What's going on?"

Joe moves forward. "What have you got there?"

Brandon steps back from him. "Photos." He swivels, so he can see me. With one brief look he tells me that he's holding something of significance. "Here's a photo of Joe and Kyra, his girlfriend who died last summer. And this is Fay with her dad, I think."

The first one is a printed version of Joe's favourite photo, him on the beach with Kyra. The other is the precious photo Fay showed me that she kept in her suitcase. It's been ripped from its silver frame. Brandon turns them over, and across the back in thick black marker pen there's writing, and someone's drawn the same weird symbol on both – something that looks vaguely familiar.

"You've been through my bag," says Joe in a calm, cold voice. "Those photos mean a lot to me so I'd appreciate you giving them back. They're none of your business."

"Hang on," says Pippa. She holds out her arm so that Joe can't go any nearer Brandon.

Brandon speaks more quickly. "They both have *Rest in Peace* and the same symbol."

Joe shakes his head in a show of exasperation. "I've just swum across a river. Can you hurry up and make your point."

"My point is," says Brandon, "I scanned that image with my phone and did a search. There's a website that uses that symbol. It's supposed to offer support to suicidal people but there's a nasty vibe to it. You wrote on Fay's photo and drew that symbol before anyone knew she was missing, didn't you?"

"I don't know what you're talking about," says Joe. "Fay gave me that photo as a present. She'd already written on it herself."

I shake my head. Fay would never have defaced the photo in that way, pressing down on the marker pen so carelessly that the ink bled through to the front, wrecking it.

"If she did it herself, then you knew what she was planning to do," says Brandon. "You must have known what that symbol was because it's on the back of Kyra's photo too. Are you telling me Kyra did that?"

"Yes," says Joe. "She did." He speaks calmly but his eyes are darting about.

I see Pippa glance at the centre director.

"Come on," says Brandon. "It's your writing, isn't it?"

The necklaces. That's where I've seen the scribbled symbol before. I stand up and whisper, "Joe made necklaces for Kyra and Fay with that symbol on. He has photos of them wearing the necklaces on his phone."

Pippa comes over and I repeat it into her ear.

"Where's your phone, Joe?" asks Pippa. She takes the photos from Brandon.

"What's going on?" asks Joe. "What are you accusing me of here?" His voice has lost its composure.

In an attempt to stop the dizziness in my head I squeeze and unsqueeze my toes.

"Skye saved Fay on her own, didn't she?" says Brandon.

My legs are wobbly but I don't sit down. I stay absolutely still so I don't miss Joe's reply.

"No," he snaps. "She didn't save her. She snatched Fay's chance to restore the balance. Skye shouldn't have interfered." He throws his mug on the ground, spraying tea in an arc over the grass. "I've had enough of this conversation."

He strides off on a path that leads to the accommodation blocks. The centre director follows him, and I hear Pippa on her phone, requesting the immediate presence of the police officer who is taking a statement from Danielle in the staffroom.

I place my own mug on the arm of the bench and make my way across to Brandon. We wrap our arms around each other, tightly, for long, comforting seconds before I whisper, "How did you know to look in Joe's bag?"

"There had to be something hidden away," says Brandon. "People like him always keep mementoes of their victims, don't they? The problem was persuading his room-mates to let me rifle through his bag. I told them I was finding him some warm clothes." He clutches my shoulders, and his expression is serious. "Listen, Skye, I'm sorry about this afternoon. What happened ... between us. I didn't mean to be patronizing, if that's what you thought, and what you told me didn't make me like you any less. I was happy you trusted me enough to tell me the truth."

I nod. It means I'm sorry too. I want to kiss him but

the inside of my mouth is too revolting, so I curl into his body for another hug, inhaling the shop smell of his shirt. My blanket drops to the ground but Brandon doesn't care that I'm wet and stink of chlorine laced with manky lake water.

After a bit, I look up at the dusk-heavy sky and think, *I saved Fay, but I'm sorry it couldn't have been you, Luisa.*

epilogue

We sit, Brandon and me, in a park near the shop that repairs phone screens. We have food for a picnic but I'm not interested in eating right now. I lean in, instead, to kiss him. He has one hand on my back, the other in my hair, and there is a fizzing inside me. A pleasure that astounds me.

Since Morley Hill, I've had fewer nightmares. When I close my eyes, I don't always see the pool of red water. I've had one panic attack. It was frightening while it lasted but it came and it went. I'm still keeping a record of them in my diary. Maybe one day I won't remember the last time I had one. Maybe they'll always be lurking. But I'm mostly calmer now, and that helps.

When our lips are numb, we stop kissing. We lie side

by side in the grass. Holding hands. I think about some of the people who've been part of my life this summer.

About Joe, who I didn't see again. We heard he was required to have an urgent psychiatric assessment, and there would be an investigation into the circumstances of Kyra and Fay's overdoses.

About Fay, who didn't die. Whose life I saved. She wrote me a note to say thank you. On paper that had a border of yellow ducks. She said she'd made a mistake. She wanted to be alive. That she was going to change schools but she still wanted to be a doctor. That her mum had taken the rest of the summer off work.

About Danielle, who showed me her video footage from the week while I was waiting to give my statement to the police, before her dad and his respite carer came to take her home. Some of it was arty. There was a panoramic sweep of the grounds that made me hit pause. She'd inadvertently caught Toby on camera, delivering crates of vegetables to the kitchen. He looked stooped. Isolated. When I returned home, I got in touch via the farm shop website. Just to say I felt able to be in contact with him again. Not super regularly or anything, but if he ever wanted to chat about Luisa I'd like that.

About Annika, whose parents invited our whole family back to Pitford for a barbecue. On the way, we drove up the track to Yew Tree House and Mum cried, but it was OK. We called in at the farm shop and bought a couple of Lower Road Farm sauces, and Dad told Toby about his new job in an office on the fifteenth floor of an office block. Annika and I sat in her bedroom that I knew so well, and while everyone else was in the garden I told her exactly what happened last summer. I'm able to say it out loud now in a normal voice. Without totally shrivelling inside. I told her what happened at Morley Hill too, and it made me feel better about myself. On the drive home, I decided to try harder at my new school to make friends.

About Brandon, who lives near enough to meet up with at weekends when term starts. He's going to Skype or send me video messages during the week. When his hand is in mine, like now, I feel happy. As happy as it's possible to be when you have a life with bruised parts in it. Which, surprisingly, is pretty darn happy.

We pack up our picnic after a while, and walk to the shop to pick up my phone. It looks like new and actually works. A minor miracle. We carry on back to Brandon's house. I lie under his white baby sister's play gym for a bit with her, seeing things from her point of view. It's a full-on experience of colour, noise and crinkly textures. His mum asks me about the running club I've joined. I tell her I like it. It helps to clear my head, and if I'm running with anyone annoying, I just plunk my earphones in, and drift into a separate world.

Later, after being up in Brandon's bedroom, where we sit on his bed and kiss some more, we save all the photos on my phone to several different places. He walks me to the train station and I take a selfie of us to start a new photo collection.

I'm still on the train with two stations to go when I see the sunset. Red and pink. Striking and dramatic. The colours are reminiscent of Luisa's nail varnish combo, and I realize there are reminders of people wherever you are if you look hard enough. I reach for my phone.

I open up MessageHound and I write a last message. **Goodbye Luisa. I love you**. And I delete the app.

acknowledgements

A thousand thanks to Becky Bagnell for her brilliant agenting skills and kindness. Thank you to Lucy Rogers, Lena McCauley and Samantha Smith at Scholastic for loving my book, and giving it an audience, and to Sean Williams for designing the perfect cover.

I'm very grateful to Catherine Johnson for steering me in the right direction when I started writing for teenagers, and Natalie Doherty for her thoughtful comments on this book.

To my writer friends, Emma Rea, Elena Seymenliyska, Ruth Jenkins, Cath Howe and Janette Simpson, who walked the hard path to publication with me – thank you for your suggestions and support.

To my parents, Robert and Elizabeth Franklin, thank you for teaching me to be true to myself, the importance of elevenses and for never censoring what I read as a child. I loved it, Mum, when you cried on hearing *Lying About Last Summer* was going to be published! Thank you to my siblings Clare and Nick for being on my side, and to so many other people who encouraged me along the way.

Richard, soulmate and resident IT consultant, thanks for being there, especially when things were tough. And for the time you dried out my laptop.

Phoebe, Maia and Sophie – thanks for generally being the Bee's Knees.

SEE

THERE'S

HOW

NO WAY

THEY

OUT

LIE

SUE WALLMAN

MAE THINKS THAT THE REASON SHE'S GROWN UP IN A PSYCHIATRIC
FACILITY IS BECAUSE HER FATHER WORKS THERE AS A DOCTOR.

IT'S NOT.